When Raoul Vincenne was murdered and five priceless diamonds were stolen, John Mannering, alias THE BARON, knew he must avenge the death.

Would Vincenne have been murdered if he had not arranged to sell the diamonds to the Baron?

When the Baron was himself kidnapped and threatened with death, his question was answered. He too was facing a ruthless gang who would stop at nothing to recover the diamonds . . .

and published by Corgi Books

John Creasey
as Anthony Morton

Versus The Baron

CORGI BOOKS
TRANSWORLD PUBLISHERS LTD
A National General Company

VERSUS THE BARON

A CORGI BOOK 552 08606 1

Originally published in Great Britain
by Sampson Low

PRINTING HISTORY
Sampson Low edition published 1940
Corgi edition published 1971
Copyright © John Creasey 1971

This book is set in 10 pt. Imprint.

Corgi Books are published by Transworld Publishers Ltd.,
Cavendish House, 57–59 Uxbridge Road,
Ealing, London, W.5.
Made and printed in Great Britain by
Hunt Barnard Printing Ltd., Aylesbury, Bucks.

Versus The Baron

Chapter 1
An Appointment of Importance

'This Mannering,' said Raoul Vincenne gently, 'he is an honest man, that I know. And wealthy, Annette. He can and will pay what is requested for so great a prize. You need have no more worries, *ma chérie*, it will not be long now before we have all the money we shall need for the great fight. Yes, the great fight – '

A pair of mild blue eyes, sparkling with feeling, regarded the petite and charming face of the girl who sat at ease on a settee in a suite at the Regal Hotel, Piccadilly. Her expression now was stormy, as if she viewed her father with impatient tolerance.

'How often our troubles have ended,' she said sharply. 'Always you find some way, and then – poof! – it goes. There was the money Richard had – where is that?'

'He will get it back, Annette, when Mannering has paid me, have no fear of that. And afterwards a bigger reward for him, for you, for me, Raoul Vincenne!'

The Frenchman flung his hands outwards, and there was fire in his eyes, the fire of the fanatic.

'A bigger reward,' Annette said sharply. 'But at what risk? All the time you are frightened, I am frightened – '

'No risk is too great, for they are mine, those lovely jewels, mine to sell to whom I wish. And' – his voice dropped to a whisper – 'no one knows what they are, Annette. This Mannering, great collector though he is, he does not know. I have been careful, Annette.'

'But you are still afraid.' The girl rose quickly, turning towards the door leading to her bedroom. 'I have to meet Richard at one o'clock, Papa. You see Mannering when?'

'At two o'clock, Annette, and in a little hour I shall be back.' His voice rose. 'If I am not here by three o'clock, then go to M'sieu Mannering and – but I shall be here! I shall start to fight, I shall prove who I am, they must acknowledge Raoul Vincenne, the one remaining descendant of – '

When Annette returned, dressed for the street, he was crouching in a deep chair, his head in his hands. She pressed her lips tightly against the back of his neck.

'The day will come, Papa, be sure of that.'

Downstairs she waited in the foyer, oblivious to the others nearby, until the swing doors opened, and a young man entered, fair-haired and tall. He reached out both hands towards her.

'Darling, it's good to see you!'

Anne laughed lightly, as he led her towards the doors.

'Papa he remains upstairs, but he will have good news quite soon. I am sure of it.'

Richard Clayton looked down at her sharply.

'Has he taken the stones?'

'Oh, yes.' Annette shrugged her shoulders.

'And he's prepared to sell right away?'

'It would seem so, Richard. This Mr Mannering is wealthy and a big collector of jewels. He –'

'I know all about John Mannering,' said Clayton confidently. 'Provided he doesn't learn that the things were stolen –'

'Stolen!' She flashed the word, luckily out of ear-shot of passers-by, for they were in Piccadilly and entering Green Park. 'How could he steal what is his? Have we to go through all that again?'

'It's possible that Mannering might not look on the matter in quite that light,' said Clayton drily. He tightened his grip on her arm. 'Forget it for an hour or two, Annette, heaven knows we don't get much time together.'

'You ask me to forget *that*,' exclaimed Annette. '*Tiens*, what is it you have for a heart?' she added slowly. 'I am to meet Papa again at three o'clock. And then – forty thousand pounds.' Her breath quickened. 'You will be repaid, and afterwards it will be proved that my father is of the proud families of France.'

'I hope to God it goes through without trouble,' said Clayton. 'Anyhow, we'll soon know.'

At ten minutes to two he watched, with a deeper interest than he allowed to show, Vincenne step from the doors of the Regal into a waiting taxi, the older man gripping a brief-case with fierce tenacity.

At five minutes to two Vincenne stepped from the taxi, paid the driver, and looked across Shaftesbury Avenue to *Mendor's*, a private club where he hoped to meet Mannering and sell to him the diamonds stowed away in his brief-case.

Vincenne glanced at his wrist-watch and saw that it was two minutes to the hour. As the traffic slowed down he stepped into the roadway.

He had no chance to save himself.

A low-slung black car leapt forward, and before he had taken two steps it crashed into him. Vincenne's body was flung five yards from the spot, and the brief-case flew in another direction. The black car went on, swerved round a bus and joined a stream of traffic.

Almost at the moment of the crash a man left the pavement and hurried towards the brief-case. If any folk nearby saw him pick it up they were too startled to make any comment or try to stop him. He slipped it beneath his coat and walked swiftly to a side-street, where a parked car was waiting for him.

The driver raised his brows interrogatively.

The man nodded, stepped into the tonneau, and was driven quietly away.

* * *

M'sieu Bon of the *Sûreté Generale* and Superintendent Lynch of Scotland Yard had two things in common. The first and obvious one was that they were policemen; the second, as obvious, was that they were fat.

Lynch had the massive roundity of an athlete who, approaching middle-age, had given up all training, while Bon, on the other hand, had the pale city face and round, tightly-waisted figure of one who abhors all sport.

On that warm afternoon in the middle of June his face shone and his lips moved with a speed that made his English difficult to follow. He lifted a plump white hand as if to stop Lynch from interrupting, an action which caused the lips of Inspector William Bristow to twitch in an amused smile.

'So!' exclaimed M'sieu Bon with fine disgust. 'The Baron, you say, is finished. For how long have you tried to find him – three, four, five years! *Nom d'un nom*, once a thief, always a thief, is it not so? I, Bon, say yes!'

Lynch, a placid man, broke in smoothly: 'You may be right, Bon, but – '

'So you will admit that?' Bon leaned forward with passion. 'Why do you not continue to look? I ask you – why?'

'We – ' began Bristow, but he was not allowed to finish.

Bon swept him aside.

'Here you have the Baron. The most notorious thief in

9

England, the most clever – the man who for four-five years laughs at you! You allow your papers to make him the hero; you have not the jewels he has stolen. How much I know not, but two-three-four hundred thousands, in pounds, is that not so? Then he stops. You say he will not work again. *Parblieu*, when he has spent all the money, *then* he starts. Always they do that. Five years ago he begins, two-three times he have a rest, only to start again. Mark the word of Bon, my friend, you make the *mistake*!'

Lynch's eyes twinkled. Bristow shifted in his chair.

'The thing is,' said Lynch easily, 'you don't know the Baron as well as we do, Bon. He's not the usual run –'

'*Nom d'un nom*, you also think him clever?'

'Not a doubt about that,' said Lynch quietly.

'It would appear,' grunted Bon, 'that you think there is not. Also that you like him!'

'He has points,' admitted Lynch, flicking a speck of ash off his coat lapel. 'Don't bother your head about the Baron, Bon, we can look after him – eh, Bristow?'

'Just now, anyhow,' said Bristow.

Bon shot a startled glance from one to the other.

'*Nom d'un nom*, you talk as if you know the man!'

Lynch chuckled.

'We do.'

'But – but *who* is he?' Bon's ebullience had dropped away from him as he stared blankly, waiting for enlightenment. 'He is a man in high places? You have the orders –'

'Oh, no, no, no! We've got some damn fool regulations, but we haven't come to that yet.'

'You – you *know* him!' said Bon in amazement, 'and – and you don't *arrest* him?'

'We haven't had a chance of getting an open-and-shut case,' said Bristow, 'and anything less is useless for the Baron. Don't look like that, man, we –'

'What do I look like?' demanded Bon sharply. 'Amazement, bewilderment, that can be allowed. *Nom d'un nom*, never shall I understand you English! All they say about you, and more, is right. We do not deal with our criminals that way in France. I –'

A tap on the door interrupted him.

Lynch called 'come in', and a sergeant entered.

'Mr John Mannering has called, sir. Can you see him?'

Bristow was taken suddenly with a fit of coughing, and

Lynch's lips curved quickly at the corners. The sergeant waited impassively, while Bon looked on, his eyes flashing from face to face.

'Er – ' said Lynch. 'He asked for me?'

'I understand so, sir, or Mr Bristow.'

'Hmm,' said Lynch. 'All right, Mason, bring him along. I'll see him here. An old friend,' he added as the sergeant went out, 'of yours, Bon. Remember the time you had a Baron burglary in Paris, and a man named Mannering was robbed of a few hundred pounds?'

'So – that Mannering?' exclaimed Bon. 'I remember well, there was a murder. You ask *him*,' he went on, wagging a finger, 'if *he* wishes the Baron to be forgotten. I – Lynch! Why do you laugh?'

Lynch recovered himself, while Bristow's face was turned carefully away from the Frenchman.

'Sorry, old man, I was thinking it would be funny to see Mannering and the Baron face to face.'

'So,' said Bon, 'you admit I am right! I – ah! M'sieu Mannering. This is a great pleasure!' He bounded towards the door as the caller was ushered in, taking Mannering's right hand between both his own. 'A great pleasure!' he repeated with conviction. 'One day, I show you a copse. You remember?'

'Copse?' asked Mannering. 'I – oh, *corpse*! Yes – Inspector Bon, isn't it?' He smiled, and for a moment was revealed as a remarkably good-looking man. 'Do I remember! I've – '

Bon did not allow him to continue, but talked without ceasing for several minutes. He, Bon, was outraged because the English police had not yet caught the Baron. He felt sure that Mannering would agree with him with equal outrage. The English, they . . . but let him not be misunderstood. For the English he had the profoundest respect. They could always take the hint. He, Bon, was French but could also take that! Messieurs Lynch and Bristow had been of the greatest kindness, and he must leave them to proceed with the matter M'sieu Mannering had come to discuss . . . but M'sieu Mannering would remember to protest, ha! ha! . . .

He shook hands warmly. As the door closed behind him, Bristow chuckled aloud, while Lynch, smiling, brushed ash from his coat.

John Mannering regarded them sardonically, his eyes alone showing that he shared their amusement. He took the chair

Bon had vacated, adjusted the fall of his trousers, and offered cigarettes from a gold case. Lynch took one, as Mannering said:

'May I share the joke, Superintendent?'

Lynch struck a match, his eyes steady above the flame.

'I rather thought you were doing so,' he said drily. 'What brings you here?'

Chapter 2
And Presents a Problem

All that Bon, Lynch and Bristow had said of the Baron had been true. That he and Mannering were one and the same, had been within an ace of being proved more than once.

Nevertheless, he had not worked for the sake of gain for over two years: which did not mean that if work should be forced on him he refused to gain by it. There had been three affairs where his powers as a cracksman extraordinary – and the police of two continents admitted those powers – had enabled him to help the police, friends of his own or Lorna Fauntley's, the girl he hoped one day to marry.

Lynch, now, pulled his chair up and nodded.

'All right, Mannering, I'm at your service.'

Bristow pulled a pad towards him, and unostentatiously took a pencil from his pocket.

'Bristow might like to make some notes,' said Mannering gently. 'All right, Bill, you'll probably need them, it's going to be involved at times. We'll start with the fact that I collect jewels.'

'You're a collector, yes – go on.'

'Well, I've had some diamonds offered to me, indirectly, and in a way that might be called dubious,' said Mannering. He had dropped his attitude of half-cynical amusement, and if Lynch and Bristow felt surprise at the opening, they concealed it well. 'The stones,' he went on, 'are fairly big, and perfectly matched. They are cut as stars, five-point stars, and are rose-tinted. I'd value them at fifteen thousand apiece – and there are five of them.'

'Just a minute,' said Lynch. 'You mean they're single stones, not small ones set into stars?'

'I mean just that,' answered Mannering. 'Each is a diamond on its own, each must have been cut down severely to make the shape, and that suggests that they're part of a collection. There are several five-star pieces in existence, I know, but none, I believe, that are missing.'

'Have you tried to find out?'

'As a matter of fact, I have. I've even cabled New York, and Paris. A blank, both times.'

'You could have contacted us a bit earlier,' Lynch said drily. 'I hope you've not made the mistake of leaving it too late.'

'I don't make that kind of mistake with Scotland Yard!' Mannering said, smiling. 'You can take it as read that they're not posted as missing.'

'Hmm. What makes you think it might interest us?'

'Method of offering,' said Mannering, and he hesitated, choosing his words carefully. 'I was at *Mendor's* four days ago, and I saw them there. A complete stranger suggested that these diamonds were rare enough to interest me no matter what awkward questions might at some time have to be asked, and – '

He broke off, while Lynch's eyes narrowed and Bristow glanced up from his notebook. Both men knew that they had not heard the full story: it was one which only a very few collectors would have brought to the Yard by itself. Lynch could have named a dozen men in public life of irreproachable reputation, and – in all matters but their collection – meticulous honesty, who possessed precious stones of dubious history. It presented the Yard with many problems: a slight adjustment in the cutting of a diamond – or emerald, ruby or sapphire – could make certain identification impossible, and explained the difficulty in tracing well-known pieces that had been stolen. Such pieces, Lynch knew, were in the Baron's collection – and that of at least one Cabinet Minister.

Even those who demanded a higher standard for their collections would hesitate to report an offer made tentatively, sometimes because of the difficulty of identification, more often because they were reluctant to endanger a source of supply.

'Well?' said Lynch.

Mannering tapped the desk lightly with his fingers.

'That in itself was unusual but not unprecedented. I had ten or fifteen minutes to examine the stones, and I was interested.'

'*Hmm*,' grunted Lynch.

'At a figure of fifty thousand, not too far from their face-value,' went on Mannering. 'All perfectly in order, Lynch, and at the moment I would certainly have been unjustified in worrying you about it – '

'But you took other precautions?'

14

'I asked for fuller particulars at my second meeting.'

Lynch shifted his position.

'When and where?'

'*Mendor's*, yesterday afternoon.'

'Did you get a straight answer?'

'I did not. I was reasoned with, and the price was knocked down by ten thousand – by which time,' added Mannering with a smile, 'I began to realise that it was a matter for the Yard.'

'Go on.'

'I accepted the offer.'

Lynch looked startled, for the first time that afternoon, and Bristow glanced up sharply from his desk. The Baron's face was expressionless and his voice lowered a fraction.

'Delivery was at two o'clock this afternoon, again at *Mendor's*. I lunched there, and waited for my man.'

'You wouldn't be telling us this if you'd got them,' grunted Lynch.

'Possibly not,' said Mannering, but although he spoke lightly there was an underlying note of seriousness in his voice. 'However, my man didn't turn up.'

'Probably as well for you.'

'But not as well for him, I'm afraid.'

Lynch leaned forward.

'Mannering, what are you getting at?'

'The reason I came to see you,' said Mannering. 'My man was, undoubtedly, French. Tall, thin, past middle-age, bearded and quite grey. He spoke good English, he seemed a member of a good family, and he was very frightened. So much so that I advanced him five thousand against the security of one of the stones, which was left in *Mendor's* safe yesterday. He wanted the money urgently, and told me that he was flying to Paris overnight but would certainly be back today.'

'He could have missed his plane,' said Lynch.

'But in fact he didn't. He was at *Mendor's* just before noon, paid five thousand pounds to Ponting, the manager there, and took the diamond away – that was arranged, if he wanted to change his mind; we would have been even on the deal, and I'd have had no complaints. However, he told Ponting that he would like to see me at two o'clock. Just why I don't know; I might have done had he stayed alive.'

Lynch stiffened, his hands gripping the arms of his chair.

'Just – what do you mean?' Lynch spoke gruffly.

'He was killed in a car smash,' Mannering said, 'half-an-hour ago. Outside *Mendor's.* I didn't see it, but heard it and saw him being put into an ambulance. The sergeant at the spot assured me that he hadn't a brief-case with him. He'd had one when he first came to *Mendor's* today, and Ponting saw him put the diamond in it. There may be nothing to it, Lynch, but the poor beggar died apparently in one of those hit-and-run smashes. He might have deposited the case somewhere between noon and two o'clock, of course, but it's as likely that he was coming back to complete the deal. The problem, I fancy, is to check up on the missing case. Agreed?'

Lynch reached for a telephone and spoke sharply:

'Get me AZ Division at once – Superintendent Buller if he's there.' He replaced the receiver and eyed Mannering without expression. 'You're right. Mannering, have you told me the unvarnished truth?'

'Even to showing myself in a jewel-collector's mysterious light,' said Mannering drily.

'No trimmings?'

'None whatever.'

'Thanks. You'll sign the statement?'

'No,' said Mannering, 'but I'll sign one which gives a bare résumé of the facts. There's one other thing, although it isn't likely to help much – the man called himself Vincenne, Raoul Vincenne.'

Lynch looked at him gravely.

'You've interested yourself in affairs not unlike this before, Mannering, and you've nearly burned your fingers. This is a job for the police, and we don't want any kind of interference. Will you bear that in mind?'

'I certainly will, Lynch. Anything else?'

'I shall probably want you for the identification.'

'I'll be at my flat, or Portland Place,' said Mannering, rising.

The Superintendent said nothing until the door had closed behind him.

'What do you make of it, Bristow?'

'There's something behind it,' said Bristow flatly.

'I'm afraid so. Better have Mannering watched – no need to start until tonight though. I – '

The telephone, with Superintendent Buller of the AZ Division at the other end, cut him short.

* * *

16

'The trouble with you, darling,' said Lorna Fauntley, 'is that you're an incurable romantic.'

Mannering coiled a tress of her dark hair about his finger. 'I was interested in Vincenne, and I liked him. I –'

'You were bored to death, and it looked like an opportunity for a spice of excitement,' amended Lorna.

'Proceed,' said Mannering lazily.

'I'm going to,' she said, and took a deep breath. 'John, why don't we face up to things, and live together? Half the world thinks we do now; it would make no difference. It's a damnable situation as it is – how can we go on like this? No wonder you're restless, reckless, unstabilised –'

'Listen, Lorna. We're waiting as we agree in the saner moments it's wiser to do. That husband of yours' – he was speaking very carefully – 'will have to fade out one day, or else you'll get a divorce. Sooner or later. And if you think sharing a flat or a country cottage regularly is going to make the slightest difference to wanting that you're all wrong, sweetheart. And if you think that getting married would stop me from getting – occasionally – interested in an affair like Vincenne's, you're just as wrong.'

'I –' She turned abruptly, and his arms went round her.

Theirs was an unbearable situation at times, tragic in its simplicity. A husband who had married her secretly, had proved himself – by his spells in prison and out – a complete rogue, a father who was a minor Cabinet Minister with high ambitions . . .

Divorce, even disclosure of the marriage, might easily ruin those ambitions, and Mannering knew that if Lorna did that she would for ever regret it. And he knew – though he had not succeeded in convincing her of this – that in the part of the Baron he found more relief than in any other outlet.

She said presently: 'Have you told the police everything you know about Vincenne?'

'Everything except that bit about a daughter. An odd story,' went on Mannering reflectively. 'She was in some kind of jam, so he said, and he had to find the money for her. Admitted that the stars weren't his, but assured me that no one would ever miss them, or look for them. That's the vital factor, Lorna, he admitted they weren't his. If he'd protested that they were, I'd have said that he pitched it well, but –' He frowned. 'The man was murdered, that's what sticks.'

'You're not sure.'

'As near as makes no difference. Oh, damn!' He broke off, at a tap on the door. 'Yes?'

'There's a lady to see you, sir.'

'To see me?' said Mannering, surprised that anyone should call at Lorna's home for him. 'You're sure?'

'Quite sure, sir.'

It was then, quite abruptly, that Mannering's decision to take a personal part in the affair of the five stars was made. There was a sharp, feminine exclamation, a masculine protest, and the quick opening of the door. A woman – little more than a girl – burst into the room; a tiny, vividly pretty thing.

'I'm Annette Vincenne!' she cried, and stepped quickly towards Mannering, her hands raised in appeal.

Chapter 3
Murder it was

'He – he told me about you.'

'Who?' smiled Mannering.

'You – you do not know him? My father – Raoul Vincenne, he saw you, he sold you the stars. It must be true.'

So she didn't know, thought Mannering; and it did not seem the moment to break bad news, for in her manner there was already tragedy enough. Yet he could not altogether convince himself that the effect of her forced entry was genuine. Like her father's story, it had a ring of truth and yet a false note that he could not identify.

'It was true, up to a point,' he said. 'Will you smoke?' She took a cigarette and tapped it nervously on a lightly polished thumb-nail. 'Just why have you come?'

'I want to know where he is!'

'Why should you expect me to know?'

'He was to meet you, yes, at two o'clock? Afterwards he was to meet me at the Regal Hotel. He did not come. Now it is nearly four o'clock, and – Mr Mannering! Did he have the money? Please answer me!'

'Supposing he did?' asked Mannering quietly. 'He –'

'He had it! And he has gone, they have found him, they –'

Mannering felt exasperation, concern, wariness.

'You're taking rather a lot for granted,' he said. 'Who do you mean by "they"?'

'The – two men. They have been following him; since he brought the stars to England they have watched him, he told me that, he was so frightened but so happy that you were going to buy them. They were his by right, yes, I –'

'I see,' said Mannering, glancing at Lorna who had retreated unobtrusively to the window. 'Two men knew that he had the diamonds and followed him, but you don't know them?'

'I? Why should I?'

It could not be put off any longer. Mannering must tell her. He said quietly:

'Miss Vincenne, your father did not arrive at the meeting place, and nothing changed hands. Certainly he had no money of mine with him.'

'He – *didn't come*? But he flew from Paris, he told me everything was arranged. He was afraid that if he had the money it would be stolen, he would be attacked. If he had not reached the Regal at three o'clock, I was to find you. You were not at your flat. I make enquiries. I come here. You *must* have seen him!'

Mannering pushed one hand deep into his pocket and said very softly:

'He has been seen, Miss Vincenne, and I'm afraid the news is bad. He met with – an accident. I – '

Annette leaned forward.

'He – is – hurt?'

'I'm sorry. I'm afraid – '

'Dead!' she screamed, and then screamed again, her mouth wide open. 'No, no, no!' She leapt from her chair. 'It can't be, you're lying, he – '

'I wish I were,' said Mannering.

For a moment she stood there, then swung round, half-running to the door.

Mannering took a quick step in her wake, then stopped as Lorna's voice came to him on a note of urgency.

'Wait, John.'

The door slammed, and they could hear the girl's footsteps as she rushed towards the landing. Lorna spoke again, this time from the window.

'She said two men. There are two outside, they've been there all the time. If you follow – '

She could feel his excitement as he turned from her, hating it yet knowing she was powerless to stop him.

Through a window on the landing Mannering saw the girl reach the street. Following her he saw that one man was walking in the wake of Vincenne's daughter, while the other was going in the same direction on the far side of the road.

There had been little time for thinking, and there was none now. The girl walked sharply as far as Oxford Street, and then stopped a taxi. The two men climbed into a Morris 8 and went ahead of the cab, while Mannering called a second cab, boarding it as it moved.

'Follow the Morris,' he said, and gave the cabby no time to answer.

He sat back, frowning a little and watching the girl's cab, trying again to reconcile her actions with her words. She had gone out, apparently bordering on hysteria, but she had been calm enough when she had called the cab and given instructions. Had she gone walking blindly it would have been easier to understand.

He heard a startled exclamation from his cabby.

At the same time the front wheels swung towards the kerb so violently that he was jolted forward. He glanced round sharply as a Talbot sports car cut sharply in. His driver, forced on to the pavement, jammed on the brakes, bellowing at the other driver as he did so. But the sports car slid between two buses, its engine purring powerfully, and beat a set of traffic lights by a split-second. Traffic closed behind the Morris and the girl's cab.

Mannering's cabby had jumped down, and wrenched open the door, livid-faced.

Mannering took his wallet out, but had no time to offer recompense before a policeman arrived, moving with the stolid haste of his kind. It was impossible, now, for Mannering to catch up with his quarry. He contrived to finish the formalities in five minutes, for there was no damage more than a shaving of paint off the taxi's wing, and then he walked slowly back towards Portland Place.

The girl, two men she feared, and the sports car, were all concerned in that quick getaway. He did not believe the Talbot had pulled in front of the cab accidentally: it seemed clear that he had been followed, and that no chance had been given him to find where the girl was going.

But had the sports car driver been working with Annette Vincenne, or with the two men?

He lit a cigarette as he neared the Fauntleys' house; and then let the match burn down to his fingers as he saw a car pulled up outside.

Bristow, he thought, and shrugged.

Bristow it was, waiting patiently for Lorna. Mannering met her crossing the hall, but there was no chance of speaking. He motioned her to go in first, and waited.

'Good afternoon, Miss Fauntley' – Bristow spoke in his most formal manner – 'I'm told Mr Mannering is here. I wonder –'

Mannering pushed the door wider open.

'Hallo, Bill, business already?'

Bristow's manner changed, grew brusque.

'Glad you're back, Mannering. I'd like you to come along for that little matter of identification, if you will.'

'All right, I won't be churlish enough to refuse.' Mannering, with a brief goodbye to Lorna, led the way to the door. Bristow appeared to have taken umbrage, and said nothing as he climbed in the police car and let in the clutch.

Mannering sat back, more than a little curious, faintly apprehensive. Bristow's manner was very much like it had been in the old days when he had imagined he had at last obtained evidence against the Baron.

As far as this affair went that was impossible.

But the uncertainty remained. Behind Mannering there was a record of cracksmanship long enough to have seen him sentenced to seven, even fifteen years' imprisonment. That the Press had called him – with some justification – a new Robin Hood would have no effect on a judge or jury.

Steady, said Mannering to himself, this is an identification, not a charge-room job. Aloud: 'You seem to be rattled, Bill.'

'*Rattled!*' snorted Bristow, pulling up with a jerk at their destination. 'Believe me, that's one of the mildest reactions you cause to us poor flatfoots.'

'Hmm,' said Mannering. 'So it's like that, is it.'

'Yes,' said Bristow, 'just like that.'

Except for a bruise on the side of the head, the face of Raoul Vincenne had not been injured. Mannering needed only a quick glance at the pale, bearded face, lined even in death with worry and anxiety.

'Well?' asked Bristow.

'There's no doubt it's the man I saw.'

'Hmm. All right, let's get out.' They left the morgue attendant to his grim charge, and went upstairs to the C.I.D. office. 'Not much doubt that it was deliberate,' Bristow said. 'The car shot across a pedestrian crossing when he was halfway over it –'

'That's hardly proof.'

'No, but listen to this. Someone on the pavement nipped across and took his bag as it fell. *That's* pretty conclusive – or isn't it enough for you?'

'Quite enough,' agreed Mannering. 'Though we don't actually know that the diamonds were in the bag –'

'It was a minute or so before two o'clock. He was coming to hand the gems over to you, and he was about half a minute's walk from *Mendor's*. If you're telling the truth, there's not much doubt about it being murder. And the only people who can remember the car looked at it three storeys up!'

'Description?'

'A long, black one – I can't get anything else.'

'You don't need to,' said Mannering. 'I've got it for you. It was a black Talbot sports, and the driver has been up to his tricks again – yes, you can have the whole story, Bill, with a little you didn't expect and probably don't deserve. But you won't appreciate it.'

'Won't I?' demanded Bristow tartly. 'Why?'

'It has far too many complications,' said Mannering. 'Not a cut-and-dried job at all, and I've a feeling you're going to need some help.'

'If you mean what I think you mean,' said Bristow, 'then, God help you!'

Such waspishness was unlike him, particularly at the start of a case and one in which the Baron's part was so far blameless.

'Just what,' he demanded, 'is the trouble?'

Bristow eyed him sombrely.

'Those stars, Mannering, were taken from the Palace of Versailles – the Louis Quinze collection – and it's only just been discovered that paste ones were substituted. You're in it deep enough by admitting you were going to buy them, so sit tight and let's have no tomfoolery.'

Mannering eyed him squarely as Vincenne's story, his daughter's insistence on her father's right to the gems, flashed through his mind. While agreeing with Bristow that this was going to be a pretty sensational affair, he felt primarily a sharp, cold anger against the Inspector for his attitude.

'So that's your attitude, is it?'

'Yes, it is.'

'If you want more help from me it had better change,' snapped Mannering. 'Another hint from you that you're going to use the Baron fable and I'll see you damned before I talk. What is it to be? Co-operation or cut-throat? Take your choice!'

Chapter 4
Visitor

Sir David Ffoulkes, Assistant Commissioner at Scotland Yard, interrupted Bristow's spoken report and looked across at Mannering.

'You don't need telling that your admitted offer to buy the stolen goods – '

'As far as I knew they weren't stolen.' Mannering hesitated, frowned, and then laughed whole-heartedly.

'Well?' said Ffoulkes coldly as Mannering stopped.

'Just when was the loss discovered at Versailles?'

'Early this morning.'

'How odd,' said the Baron musingly. 'I telephoned Galinet that the stars were remarkably like the Louis Quinze gems, and he assured me they were in their case. I wonder if he made a closer inspection and saw enough to advise the Sûreté?'

Ffoulkes stared.

'Galinet did tell them they were paste – '

'Well, well,' said Mannering, 'you must admit it's rather funny. Through me the loss was discovered, through me you know the stars are in England, through me you find an accident that turns out to be murder; and the best thing you can do is to threaten me with action for thinking of buying stolen gems!' His anger had gone like a puff of wind, and there was an amused gleam in his eyes as he regarded the Assistant Commissioner.

Ffoulkes cleared his throat.

'We appear to be indebted to you, certainly, Mannering, and we will be further indebted if you tell us what you know about the sports car which killed Vincenne.' Ffoulkes' dry manner meant capitulation, that hostility – if not put altogether aside – was for the moment shelved.

Mannering told his story, while Bristow again took notes and Ffoulkes asked an occasional question. At the end the Assistant Commissioner rubbed his chin.

'Can you give us a description of the girl?'

'She was certainly distinctive enough to remember. Not

more than five feet high, impressive blue eyes, small bones and delicately made, very dark hair with a blueish tint, black dress with white trimmings, and a very Parisien black hat – enough?'

'It'll do, thanks. Have a call put out at once, Bristow.'

Bristow went out, and Ffoulkes straightened the pencils on the desk in front of him, while looking squarely at Mannering. 'John, we know each other pretty well, and we don't need to talk about the Baron. But keep out of this.'

'Certainly words of wisdom,' said Mannering. 'Thing is, David, I took a liking to Vincenne – '

'Or his daughter?'

'No, the daughter puzzles me. And when all's said and done Vincenne was murdered trying to see me – that gives me a certain responsibility, I think. Speaking quite frankly, I'm not unused to – investigating, shall we say? – and I may have means which you lack of getting to the bottom of this business. Any risk I'm taking is my risk, any benefit therefrom will be either for you or the girl. Do you follow me?'

Ffoulkes smiled wryly.

'Only too well. I'm tempted to say "carry on". If I could be sure that Mannering would do all the investigating, I would do so. But at the first mention of the Baron – ' He broke off and shrugged. 'You understand?'

'Perfectly,' said Mannering. 'You've made your point, David, it's a pity we're generally at cross-purposes. However, I – '

The door opened abruptly.

Into the room came Inspecteur Bon, his round face filled with several varying expressions, his little grey eyes ablaze.

'So, M'sieu, I have heard of the robbery, yes! Paris telephones me and tells me to come, and I am here! The stars of Louis, they are in England! M'sieu, they must be found. M'sieu, I demand, I ask, I *beg* you to remember what I said. I can only repeat – find the Baron, and you are likely to find the stars.' He swung round on Mannering, excitement in his eyes. 'That is so, M'sieu? *You* will agree?'

'It could be,' Mannering assured him.

Ffoulkes cut in quickly.

'We're very happy to have your co-operation.' Bon smiled, bowing as one receiving due homage. 'Why should you suggest the Baron?'

Bon looked aghast.

'*Parbleu*, why? Who else, M'sieu, could do such a thing –

it is a robbery on the biggest lines, the kind the Baron does while he laughs at laws. In so great a crime, look always for the cleverest thief.'

He listened while Ffoulkes outlined the case, frowning with abstract attention until the name Vincenne was mentioned. At that he jumped.

'Vincenne! Raoul Vincenne, yes?'

'Do you know him?'

'Know him!' gasped Bon. 'Is he not the Pretender? Does he not claim to be the direct descendant of Louis Quinze? It is what you call the hallucination. I know him well, he has worried most people of importance, and at times becomes a nuisance. Vincenne would not steal the diamonds, you can be sure, but he might have inspired the theft.'

Mannering felt Ffoulkes's eyes on him and knew that the Assistant Commissioner was feeling as intrigued as he.

So Vincenne believed that he was a descendant of Louis Quinze; that would explain his daughter's assertion in his right to the stars.

'Where is he?' demanded Bon sharply.

'If he's the man we think,' said Ffoulkes, 'he was killed in a street accident and robbed of the stars. Yes, he had them with him, they were offered to Mr Mannering. I – '

Bon listened with frequent interruptions. At the end of it, Mannering was almost sorry to go.

All idea of keeping clear of the affair had gone.

* * *

Lorna was dining with friends of her family, whom Mannering knew well enough to want to avoid. He went from the Yard to his flat, a service apartment in Clarges Street, and after an early dinner, sat down to think things out.

As he saw it:

1. Vincenne believed he had a right to the stars, needed money for his daughter (the reason for that was unknown) and had contrived to get the diamonds.
2. If Bon's estimate of the man was right, and it certainly coincided with Mannering's, Vincenne had not been the type to commit a burglary.
3. Therefore he had employed others.
4. Reasonably, it could be assumed that these others were the men who had followed Annette, and the driver of the Talbot.

5. As reasonably, Vincenne had persuaded them to get the stars. They had handed them over to him, to keep 'hot' stones out of their hands, but had trailed him to make sure that when he sold them they had their share or more.

'All of which is perfectly logical,' mused Mannering, 'until we come to the fact that *before* he received the money for them they killed him. Either someone else wanted the stars, or they changed their mind about letting him sell them. Yes, a problem. I – '

Brrrh-brrrh!

He looked at the telephone with distaste.

The caller was not likely to be Lorna, who would be in the middle of dinner.

The telephone rang again.

Resigned, Mannering moved over to the receiver and picked it up. His body stiffened as Annette Vincenne's clear, unmistakable voice came to his ear.

'M'sieu, this is to say forget me! I lost my head, it is not important, I did not right in coming. Forget, please, promise to forget!'

'That isn't easy,' said Mannering evenly. 'Are you sure you're quite all right, or – '

'It is so! Speak to no one, please, always you have my gratitude for doing that! *Please!*' There was anguish in her voice, and Mannering could imagine the appeal in her vivid eyes. He could imagine, too, that this call was inspired by fear. 'Mr Mannering, promise me, I – '

'I'd like to talk to you,' said Mannering.

'No, no! It – '

Then her voice stopped abruptly, and there was the sharp click of the receiver being replaced at the other end of the wire. He acted quickly, replacing the receiver, lifting it again and dialling O.

'Police speaking,' he said brusquely. 'I've just received a call, try to trace it please, and report to me at this number – Mayfair 81221.'

'I'll put you through to the Supervisor.'

'I – ' began Mannering, but the operator had gone. He frowned as he waited impatiently, a dozen questions coming fast upon each other.

But he did not speak to the Supervisor.

For a voice came from behind him, a smooth, suave voice in

27

which he might have imagined the faintest of French accents, even while it came with so devastating unexpectedness.

'*Replace it, Mannering. Turn round – slowly.*'

He hesitated for a second and then obeyed.

A man, considerably short of medium height, was standing by the door. Chin, mouth and nose were covered by a scarf, while in a gloved right hand an automatic was held steadily.

* * *

The pause lasted perhaps ten seconds, and then Mannering said lightly:

'An unexpected pleasure, my friend. Do you need that gun?'

'I think so, yes. That was the Vincenne girl?'

Lying was useless.

'Yes.'

'You are wise to be frank. Why did you follow her this afternoon?'

'I was interested.'

'In her or her father?'

Mannering gripped the front of his coat with his left hand, and the gun moved a fraction, but the intruder offered no unnecessary warning.

'Strictly speaking, in neither,' Mannering said pleasantly. 'I was interested in the stars.'

He had pierced the other's guard, a sharp intake of breath proved it.

'So. It was your enquiry that made Galinet ask to inspect them. But for you there would have been none of this trouble. You have much to answer for.'

'Am I supposed to apologise?' enquired Mannering.

'You are advised to speak more carefully. I see you as an accomplished liar, having heard your conversation with Annette Vincenne.'

'It's good to know I have accomplishments,' said Mannering easily. 'May I smoke, or do you object?'

'If there are cigarettes in sight, yes. Move backwards towards the table, and do not be foolish.'

Mannering obeyed, and a match flickered. He contemplated the man coolly enough, but his mind was teeming with questions – the most important being the reason for this call.

The other seemed to sense it.

'I came for two reasons, Mannering. To persuade you not to interest yourself in Vincenne's death. I have heard, of course, of your practices – '

He paused, and Mannering's heart leapt. 'Your practices.' Was the man hinting that he knew him as the Baron? That possibility, the chance that others did know, or guess, was always at the back of his mind. Fear was never far away.

'Practices?'

'You are an amateur detective, I understand.' The words held a touch of insolence.

Mannering breathed more easily: the allusion was evidently aimed at the occasions when he had contrived to help the police.

'So,' the man went on, 'it will be safer I think – you realise, of course, the safety will not apply equally? – that you accompany me on a short journey.'

Mannering stared, genuinely startled.

'I have a car and two men waiting downstairs,' the man went on. 'If it is necessary I will shoot. You will not want that to happen.'

'I'd other ideas about my future, certainly,' said Mannering.

'Excellent. You will come just as you are, and you will go downstairs, enter the car, and remember that all the time you are covered by a gun.'

The man's precise diction might have seemed theatrical, had it not held a note of grim earnestness. The audacity of the *coup* was appalling; Mannering was in the middle of London, a foot from a telephone that would bring help within five minutes, and yet he was defenceless, and knew he would have to go.

'Nicely arranged,' he said.

'Don't try to disturb the arrangements.'

The man motioned Mannering to go ahead before slipping the scarf from his face. In single file they descended the stairs.

The car, a Morris saloon and chauffeur driven, was waiting, with two men standing by it. One opened the door, and Mannering got in. His captor followed, one of the waiting men made a third in the tonneau, while the other sat next to the driver. The car started off smoothly, with no crashing of gears.

Presently the gunman's low voice cut the silence.

'Put these on, Mannering.'

He was holding something out with his left hand, and in that moment Mannering had an almost overwhelming temptation to make an effort to get away. The car had slowed down in front of traffic lights, and in ten seconds he could win or lose. It seemed incredible that they would dare to shoot or raise a commotion there, with a hundred people passing every minute, and under the eyes of at least three policemen.

Something poked into his ribs, from the second man. A cold and deadly reminder to think again. He stretched out for what the gunman offered, and found it to be a pair of spectacles. He raised them to his eyes, and as he did so blackness descended, for the glass – if glass it was – was black. He was blinded effectively, yet another reason for acknowledging the ruthless efficiency of the men he was fighting.

The car moved on, twisting and turning right and left until even with his thorough knowledge of London Mannering could not be sure where he was. And then above the din of traffic he heard the deep, unmistakable tone of Big Ben.

Westminster Bridge, then, at eight o'clock precisely.

He felt the tyre go over the tram-lines, which meant that the car was travelling towards Lambeth and Waterloo. At the end of the bridge they turned right, then left and left again. The car stopped.

Mannering was led steadily across the pavement, straight into a room, or hall, and then to a lift. He waited for the movement, and knew that he was going down.

From the lift he was led along a short passage. A door opened. Voices stopped suddenly – a man and a woman's. The door shut, while a hand removed his glasses so suddenly that under the brightness of the light he could not, immediately, take in his surroundings.

A voice said: 'So you brought him?'

The words were followed by a short laugh which did nothing to reassure Mannering. The pale blue eyes of a large man in evening dress looked into his own. His features – hard and prominent – were ordinary enough; it was his eyes, set deep beneath a slanting forehead, that fascinated the Baron. Here, he knew, was the origin of the ruthlessness he had faced, would have again to face.

'Better have a drink, you may need it,' the other said and laughed again. 'Whisky, brandy, anything you like.'

'Under the circumstances, perhaps coffee would be best,' said Mannering easily.

The man laughed with genuine humour this time.

'All right, ring for coffee, Minx, we'll see if we can handle this matter socially. Mannering, you've rather butted in, you know, but that needn't come between us. All I want from you is to know where the stars are. And take my advice, don't try to bluff me.'

Mannering strove to hide the effects of this shock. For these were the men he had believed had stolen the stars of Louis from Vincenne –

And their leader was asking him where they were.

Chapter 5
Grunfeld

The unexpectedness of the man's words snatched Mannering's attention from other things in the room. He had glimpsed
a woman, but all he had taken in was that she was dressed in a
wine-red evening gown, and that her hair was dark. For the
rest, he was conscious only of those light, frosty blue eyes.

They stared at Mannering for fully twenty seconds, then
the big man broke the silence.

'I hope you heard?'

'Perfectly,' said Mannering. 'I'm trying to believe you
mean it.'

'I shouldn't let that worry you, I'm not talking for amusement.'

'No, I'd gathered that.' Mannering spoke drily. 'The
situation's a little abnormal, isn't it? Or have I been misled by
the unexpected journey?'

'I don't like riddles,' the big man said evenly, 'and I asked
a straightforward question, Mannering.'

'Right,' said Mannering, 'then accept a straightforward
answer. I've no ideas where the stars are.' He stepped to a
table and took a Virginia 3 from a cigarette box and a pull-
match from a stand close by. 'Couldn't I know your name?
Or a name?'

Unexpectedly the big man laughed.

'You're cool, I will say that for you. You can call me
Grunfeld if you want to call me anything.'

'Oh, I can think of plenty of names to call you, but one may
as well be conventional.'

'Conventions have their moments,' the big man said
deliberately, 'but this isn't one of them. I want the stuff
Vincenne had, Mannering, and I want it badly. I'm not going
to stop at trifles to get it. I – '

Mannering laughed.

'It seems our definition of trifles isn't quite the same. The
truth of the matter, however, is this. Vincenne was bringing
the stars at two o'clock this afternoon, but he didn't turn up.

He was deliberately run down by a Talbot – not unknown to you, I believe – and murdered. The stars, with his case, were stolen then, and I took it for granted that it was in conjunction with the murder.'

Grunfeld pursed his lips.

'You make it sound convincing,' he admitted, 'or nearly so. Of course all that happened, and I have Vincenne's case, there's no argument about that.'

Mannering stared.

'Empty?'

'No. Paste.'

'*Paste*,' repeated Mannering, the word barely audible. 'No, I can't believe Vincenne was going to try to put that over me. I *saw* the stars, and there wasn't a shadow of doubt about them being genuine stones – I even advanced him five thousand on one, but he reclaimed it. Look here, Grunfeld, what do you know about this business? How did you get in touch with Vincenne? Damn it, there's a reasonable answer to it somewhere, and these things aren't toys.'

Grunfeld hesitated, and then said with the casualness of one mentioning the state of the weather:

'I must tell you that Legrand, the man who brought you here, looks after me like a father. He's a clever little man, and a very good shot. Quite ruthless, too.'

'Not alone in that, I fancy,' said Mannering evenly. 'Do I take it that you believe me?'

'More or less. Do you know, Mannering, I've a feeling we're going to get on.'

'Even that might happen,' Mannering retorted. 'Trouble is, I don't like murder. Nor, as a rule, murderers.'

Grunfeld shrugged.

'As you like. Ah, here's the coffee. Let me introduce you to Minx.'

She was still in the wine-red evening gown. Her skin, Mannering noticed, was of the creamy flawlessness found so often in dark women, and she had a figure that was superb. But for a mouth that was lifted a little on the left side, and a slight scar at that corner, she would have been beautiful. Her eyes had an unnatural brilliance – a doped brilliance, Mannering judged – and her nostrils were white, as sure an indication of a drug addict as Mannering knew.

'How are you?' Her voice was attractive. 'Coffee white or black?'

'Faintly white,' said Mannering, and tried to convince himself that this was really happening, that he had been brought to this underground apartment with a gun at his back.

The big man regarded him quizzically.

'Rather a pity you have this thing about murderers, isn't it? You don't know where you are, of course, but you *have* seen me, and Legrand – and we mustn't forget Minx. You're in touch with the police, too. You see?' His eyes did not leave Mannering's, who sipped his coffee casually enough, but with his nerves suddenly at concert pitch.

'I see. More murder?'

'Frankly,' said Grunfeld, 'I don't see any other way out. There's Legrand to consider, and he's cautious as well as efficient. On the other hand – '

'Carry on,' said Mannering. Each of the softly uttered words fell vividly on his mind. The logic of Grunfeld's attitude was undeniable, but it was difficult to believe that he was facing a man who could discuss murder – his, Mannering's, murder – with such equanimity.

'On the other hand,' repeated Grunfeld, 'supposing – let us say – you were to co-operate with us. There would be certain advantages. You could, for instance, run with the hare as well as the hounds. Merely a suggestion, of course.'

Mannering smiled, reminiscently. As the Baron, he had worked both ways, unworried by conscience, easily enough.

But Grunfeld had admitted murder.

Here was a battle of wits, a struggle that would centre about the stars of Louis, but in the background there would always be the memory of Vincenne's pale, trouble-worn face, and the death he had met.

'As a suggestion,' he said with an effort, for he knew well enough that a too-ready acceptance would invite trouble, 'it's out, I'm afraid.'

Grunfeld rubbed the side of his thick nose. Despite his English voice and clothes, there was something Teutonic about him, thought Mannering; somewhere not far back in his ancestry there was German blood.

'Hmm. Think it over. We'll have to persuade him, eh, Minx?'

The girl laughed, lightly and pleasantly.

'He doesn't look as if he'd throw his life away easily, Lew. What do you make of us, Mr Mannering?'

'Oh, something very definite as to Grunfeld and Legrand.

34

You, on the other hand, don't fit in so easily,' Mannering answered pleasantly.

'Believe me, I do.' She was mocking him, her eyes flashing brilliant. Too b illiant; they worried him.

Grunfeld looked from one to the other.

'You're clever, Mannering. Don't make a decision too soon. There aren't many collectors in the world who would refuse to have the stars of Louis in their safe, even if they couldn't be displayed. And if you help us to find them, you can have them at a reduced rate.' He chuckled. 'What did Vincenne ask?'

'Fifty, and accepted forty.'

'Indeed? I told him to ask for – ' Grunfeld stopped short, and his lips tightened. He said harshly: 'We've wasted too much time already. I can use a reliable contact with the Yard, Mannering – *reliable*, I said – and it's your one chance of staying alive. I'll give you twelve hours to think it over. But don't make the mistake of thinking you could lie to me. If you come in, you'll have to commit yourself some way the police wouldn't approve – these things can be arranged. I advise you think hard.'

He stood up with quick finality, and pressed a bell-push. Legrand entered.

'Take him downstairs,' said Grunfeld, and his manner now was harsh and Teutonic. 'Put him in Room 3, under permanent guard. Then come back here, I want to talk to you.'

Mannering was shepherded from the room. The last impression he had was of Minx's eyes, turned towards him; it seemed to him – rightly or wrongly – that she was trying to send a message.

*　　*　　*

The room into which Mannering was ushered was reasonably well-furnished as a bedroom.

'The only way out's through the door,' Legrand told him sharply. 'Don't try to take it without being told.'

Alone, Mannering turned over in his mind the recent interview.

Yes, Grunfeld could make mistakes –

But Mannering knew that his chances of taking advantage of them were small.

He was as helpless as if Bristow had at long last caught him red-handed – but with a more remorseless judge and no jury. God! What a situation!

Just for a moment he felt panic rising within him, a panic unlike anything he had experienced before. It was the absolute hopelessness of the situation, the knowledge that the organisation he had glimpsed had closed every loophole. And less than two hours before he had been sitting at ease in an armchair, not a care in the world.

He heard himself laughing, and stopped short.

Thoughts were revolving in his mind, odd facts were intruding. Part at least of his theories had been right; Vincenne had employed Grunfeld to get the stars. That was definite. But why had Grunfeld tried to get hold of them again, after handing them over to the Frenchman?

What had Vincenne been doing with paste stones?

He could find no satisfactory answer to that.

The most likely solution was that Vincenne had been robbed and the dummies substituted. Yet it was difficult to believe that anyone but himself, Annette and Grunfeld had known he had the gems in his possession. Grunfeld had not been talking for nothing, it had not been him.

Annette?

'No,' said Mannering aloud, 'that would be too obvious and too easy. Besides, the girl was scared to death, and she had no idea of her father's death. There must be someone else, or Grunfeld has a traitor in his camp.'

He laid full-length on the bed, his mind going monotonously round and round the same circle. Soon, he slept.

A faint sound awakened him.

He was alert in an instant, lying without movement, shamming sleep.

Only a glimmer of light came through the door as it opened. Into his mind flashed the possibility that Grunfeld had changed his mind, that this was to be murder –

And then he saw Minx, the light gleaming on the silken dressing-gown wrapped closely about her.

Chapter 6
Minx

Mannering's breathing did not alter. Steady and rhythmic, it seemed to be that of a man in a deep sleep, and nothing the woman did suggested that she suspected otherwise. The room was now in pitch darkness. But for her regular breathing he might have believed the whole episode to be a dream. Then from close by his head he heard the light tap of fingers against metal, and knew she was searching for the light switch by his bed.

The light came on, and he stirred deliberately. There was a pause, and then a hand touched his forehead. He stirred again, and turned over. The pressure of her fingers increased.

He started up.

'*You?* What the devil – '

Minx said softly: 'Do keep your voice down. Lew – Grunfeld – doesn't know I'm here. He won't be back until morning. Don't worry.'

'Worry!' ejaculated Mannering. 'I – '

'Do be quiet.' She made no protest as he swung his legs to the floor and stood up, but took his place, her head resting on the pillows. Her dressing-gown fell open at the neck, deliberately he suspected. 'You're rather a fool, aren't you? If you'd handled Lew differently he would still feel friendly. Instead you'll have to work hard to make him keep that offer open.'

'It's the last thing I'll do,' said Mannering sharply.

'I hope it isn't.'

'I don't see that it affects you.'

'Don't you?' she said softly.

His voice came harshly: 'I see that Grunfeld sent you here, to persuade me to stay. No, my dear, it won't work, I hate to disillusion you but I'm not at all impressed.'

Her smile disappeared, and her expression became thoughtful, almost wary.

'Don't you realise that you haven't a hope – unless you work with Lew? A life more or less won't worry him, and if he lets Legrand finish you, his position would be the same.'

Mannering said nothing and a note of pleading crept into her voice.

'I'd much rather you didn't die. After all, what does it matter if you help him? Everything's justifiable in self-defence. And – we could have some good times.' Her eyes were sparkling, her breath coming quickly in effervescent excitement.

Mannering said stiffly: 'Thanks for the invitation, but there are good times and good times, Minx, and I'm not in a bargaining mood. If it had been just the stars I might have said yes, but Vincenne was murdered, you don't seem to appreciate that. Probably others, too: Grunfeld seems a pretty ruthless swine.'

'Stop being a prude and come and lie down. If you're going to be obstinate with Lew this is your last night on earth. Why not enjoy it?'

He stood staring at her for a moment, his eyes narrowed and very hard.

'You came here to help me?'

'To try.'

'You can if you will, but not this way.'

She frowned petulantly.

'What are you getting at?'

He said abruptly: 'You know this place well. I'm wealthy enough to be able to make you comfortable for life if you tell me how to get out.'

She shook her head slowly.

'No, that's impossible. I daren't do it. You don't know Lew.' A tremor ran through her body, and for the first time he realised that she was afraid – deathly afraid – of Grunfeld. But she shook the spasm off quickly. 'In any case, I couldn't. All the outside doors are controlled by electricity, and Lew and Legrand are the only two who know just how to operate the switches.'

Mannering saw her eyes move towards the door, and felt the sudden tension of her body. Fear far greater than he had seen before showed in her face; in a flash she looked older, haggard, terrified. He swung round, but even before he saw the man he knew that Grunfeld had entered unheard.

He was standing in the open doorway, and his face was like a mask. Only his eyes showed any expression, and they were filled with cold fury.

Behind him was Legrand and a second man. They moved

quickly: Mannering was forced back, with a gun at his stomach, while Grunfeld stepped slowly towards the girl, and struck her sharply across the face.

The report of the blow was like a pistol shot, a second came, a third. She tried to turn away, but with his left hand he held her wrists together, then struck again. Hardly a muscle of his square, livid faced moved.

'You – little – '

His hand moved back, and Mannering felt his blood rising, felt a blind, ungovernable fury.

'Grunfeld, that's enough!'

'Quiet,' snapped Legrand, and the muzzle of the automatic pressed harder against Mannering's stomach. Mannering hesitated, his limbs tensed; but Grunfeld's fit of passion seemed to have been broken by the interruption, and he stood back breathing hard through parted lips.

'I'll deal with you later, you slut,' he growled, 'you can have a week in this room as you're so fond of it, but you'll be alone, and you'll have just enough to keep you alive, no more. Get him out, Legrand, and use the river – it's all he's fit for.'

Suddenly the girl started screaming, high-pitched piercing shrieks that hurt the ears. She flung herself forward, grovelling at Grunfeld's knees, and the only word Mannering heard was:

'*No, no, no!*'

'Shut up,' snarled Grunfeld. 'I – '

And then Mannering acted.

His elbow was no more than three inches from Legrand's chin, and he jerked it upwards as the man's eyes were turned towards Grunfeld and the girl. Legrand's teeth snapped together and he staggered back, while Mannering leapt towards Grunfeld. The big man's back was towards him; but the other man with a gun touched the trigger.

Mannering sent up a brief prayer of thankfulness that he had taken the precaution of wearing a bullet-proof waistcoat. The bullet struck him beneath the shoulder blade, sending a sharp, agonising pain through him, which almost paralysed his left arm; but it did not stop him moving.

In a second he was on Grunfeld, his right hand gripping the other in a half-Nelson that brought a grunt of pain from Grunfeld's lips. Mannering cared nothing for it, cared little if he broke the other's arm. He put all he knew into the pressure, forcing Grunfeld's body into a complete cover from frontal attack. He could see neither of the men, although the girl was in plain view, kneeling against the bed.

The white heat of his rage had gone, and he was estimating the situation, knowing the desperation of the chance he had taken. Slipping his right hand into his trouser pocket, his fingers caught at the knife there – a pocket knife with a four-inch blade. Slowly he drew it out, opening the blade with his teeth. He pressed the point lightly against Grunfeld's neck.

Legrand drew a deep breath, off his balance for the first time.

'If you do –'

'You'll do exactly as I tell you,' snapped Mannering, 'or this goes right in. Move back towards the dressing-table. Both of you. Then put your guns on the floor – gently does it.'

The men obeyed.

'Set your safety catch,' Mannering said. 'You Legrand. Right. Now throw it along the carpet, where Grunfeld can reach it. A false move and Grunfeld pays for killing Vincenne earlier than he expected. This isn't a game, I'm dead serious.'

The air was charged with tension, but Mannering knew that while Grunfeld's life was threatened he had a chance – a faint chance – of getting through.

The gun slithered across the carpet to within a foot of Grunfeld. Mannering said:

'Pick it up – slowly, I'm bending with you. That's right – hold it behind you.'

Grunfeld obeyed, using his free arm. As Mannering snatched the gun, slipping the safety catch back sharply, he saw Legrand move.

He fired.

The automatic was silenced, but there was a sharp sneezing sound and a foot-long stab of flame. Legrand gasped and clutched at his left arm.

Pushing Grunfeld before him Mannering reached the door, his automatic covering all three men and the girl – not that he feared trouble from her. He was breathing hard, but there was a fierce exultation in his mind, for the moment of greatest danger was gone. He stood against the door, from where he could shoot if necessary along the passage, and said more evenly:

'The other gun – pick it up and toss it to me, but put the catch back first.' He spoke to the second gunman, who obeyed quickly and without fuss. Mannering caught the gun and slipped it into his pocket.

'Thanks,' he said. 'No, Grunfeld, I won't work with you. And it will be very ill-advised to worry Minx too much.'

He heard an oath from Grunfeld as he pulled the door to and locked it sharply.

No one was in the passage.

He took the key out, and went down on one knee to examine the lock. He saw at once that it could be opened with a skeleton-key in thirty seconds, with any piece of thin wire in two or three minutes.

He slipped a handful of coins from his pocket, took a shilling, and found that vertically it almost went inside the keyhole. He wrapped a handkerchief about the butt of an automatic and knocked the shilling in, lodging it so tightly that it would be impossible to shift without a tool. Neither key nor wire would open the door now; it would have to be broken down or the lock sawn away.

He had gained time, but the main problem remained: escape from a virtual fortress. He stepped quickly towards the right, for to the left was a dead end, and reached the bottom of the flight of stone steps.

He started to go up, a hand on the rail bracketed to the wall. Halfway along, his fingers felt a slight protuberance, and he paused. If there was electric control, this might be part of it. He pressed the knob gently, heard no sound, and frowned.

His frown cleared.

At his side the wall was gaping a little, and the gap widened; inches grew into feet! When there was room for a man to pass, it stopped. The light on the steps was poor, and Mannering could see only a black void beyond the opening.

Pausing, undecided, he heard the sharp echo of approaching footsteps, and the mutter of voices.

'Room 3, wasn't it? There's enough of them to manage one bloke, I should think. I – '

Mannering stopped to hear no more; he realised that there was a bell-push in the room where he had imprisoned Grunfeld, knew that it was touch and go whether he got away. Quickly he stepped into the passage he had discovered, but as he went he heard a voice raised in sharp alarm.

'What's that? Here – hurry!'

And he knew he had been seen.

Chapter 7
Dark Journey

The brief minutes of respite from tension had given Mannering back the self-control that had nearly gone when he had been in Room 3. He had not expected to escape without trouble, and now the trouble had come he was cool enough, with the coolness the Baron had been forced to cultivate. He went forward over a slippery but even floor, making ten yards or more before he heard a voice coming as if from a long way off.

'Come out of there!'

The man would be faced with the impenetrable darkness Mannering had seen from the steps, that was certain. He hurried on, a gun in his right hand, but only to be used in acute emergency.

'*Come out!* If you don't –'

The voice sounded further away, suggesting the owner of the voice had not as yet entered the passage. Mannering paused, to slip off his shoes. The floor struck cold against his feet, but he could move without making a noise. The darkness was absolute, and he felt for the wall, finding it clammy and wet to his touch. With that to direct him he hurried along. For there would be no chance if he went back, and unless the passage led him to an exit there was no chance at all. He felt a gnawing dread in his mind that he would come to a door or an obstacle he could not pass, but he forced it aside.

Footfalls echoed behind him: one man at least was following.

He quickened his pace, but only for a moment, for he struck something which he knew he should have expected, although not for a moment had he dreamed of it. *Water!* In two steps he was ankle deep, in three the water rose almost to his knees.

The river!

It was a sewer or an outlet of some kind, and his mind flew to Grunfeld's words: 'Take him to the river, it's all he deserves.' A moment of panic assailed him again, the utter

42

darkness was itself enough to unnerve him, and he stopped for a moment, breathing hard. Stopping, he heard the lapping of the water and the approaching footfalls. He fancied that there was a slight break in the darkness behind him, and suddenly the bright ray of an electric torch shone out.

He could see nothing beyond it, but the beam ran along the surface of the water, making odd, shifting reflections. It missed him by inches, but when it drew nearer he would be right in its path.

Mannering drew a deep breath and stepped forward. Suddenly the water rose above his knees, the slimy, slippery surface beneath his feet threatening to make him lose his balance. He stopped again, pressed close against the wall, with the glow of the torch-light casting weird shadows about him. He took his wallet and some papers from his coat pocket, slipped them into his trousers, made sure the coat was empty, and dropped it. Then he stripped both waistcoats, the chained steel which had saved his life falling with a dull plop into the water. He kept both guns.

Suddenly the light bathed him, casting his own shadow on the murky water.

He heard a sharp 'There!' and almost on top of it the echo of a muffled report from a silenced gun. A bullet smacked against the wall at his side, a second and third. A fourth went over his head. He touched his own trigger twice in quick succession, risking making a silhouette against the flashes of blue flame. He seemed hardly to have fired when the torch went out, and he heard a shout from the man who had been holding it. The clatter as it fell came to his ears like the sound of breaking glass.

But it brought only temporary relief.

The impossibility of going back he accepted, the risks and chances of moving forward had to be taken quickly. Two steps found him waist deep, and then the floor of the passage either dipped steeply or disappeared, for he went under abruptly, thick, evil-smelling water rushing to his lips and nose.

He came up without struggling, drew a deep breath, and began to swim forward, his strokes long, powerful and considered.

He had no idea how many shots were sent after him, but their echoes had finished before he saw the reflection of another torch on the water. He was still within easy shooting distance, and he quickened his stroke. Five yards on, his hand hit against the roof of the tunnel.

A sharp pain made him ignore the deeper meaning for a moment, but then that flooded his mind. If the tunnel was filled to the roof, further on, there could be no escape.

No escape –

There was a stiff current running from behind him, irregular but the only thing that offered hope. He felt himself carried along at a greater speed than he could swim, for the current quickened. Twice he was buffeted against the wall, once his head touched the roof as he lifted it out of the water; in a matter of seconds he would know the worst. He needed to make no effort, for the current carried him. There was a ceaseless drumming in his ears; the pressure at his chest grew more insistent, would soon be unbearable.

He felt himself going down, felt the rush of the water completely submerge him.

He could hold on no longer. The end was very near –

Then suddenly he felt himself flung *upwards.* He went under again, but now he struck out more firmly although barely conscious. And when his head came above water for the second time he could see a thousand reflections on the broad surface of the Thames, could hear the murmur of traffic and the lapping of the water against a barge close by him.

He reached the barge and clung to it, gulping in the cool night air, physically exhausted and mentally numbed, but safe.

Safe! And he dared rest.

After a while he clambered painfully over the side of the barge, lying inert, exhausted, barely alive on the soft sand with which it was loaded, while the stars looked down on him.

*   *   *

'It isn't likely he got through,' said Grunfeld harshly, 'but have his flat, and the girl Fauntley's house, watched. Let me know if there's any word of him. You're sure he'd no idea how you brought him here?'

'None,' said Legrand, tight-lipped.

'Keep a close watch upstairs, to report anything that might be suspicious – not that there will be, he's dead all right.'

'It would have been better had we seen him die,' said Legrand, with cold conviction. 'There was no need to keep him.'

Grunfeld's light eyes met and held the black ones of the

gunman. They shared the knowledge that Legrand was right, he had made a mistake in offering Mannering terms.

He said arrogantly: 'There was a chance, Legrand. Don't confuse your job with mine.'

'It is mine to eliminate risk,' said Legrand.

They were sitting in the room which Mannering had first seen, a decanter of whisky at Grunfeld's side.

'Hmm. All right. Have a new lock fitted to Number 3, and put Minx back in there. Well – what are you staring at?'

Legrand said: 'She won't stand a week of it. Do you want to kill her?'

Grunfeld laughed, the harsh, threatening laugh Mannering had heard.

'She'll take two or three days, and she won't make that kind of mistake again. The bitch! Understand she's not to have anything, not a sniff of it. Clear?'

'You make it clear enough.'

As Legrand went out, Grunfeld followed him, stopping at a door marked '2'.

Minx was lying on a bed, her eyes closed.

'Don't do anything silly,' Grunfeld snapped, 'and you'll have your stuff again in four days. Understand, four days. Every time you're troublesome will add a day to it.'

She shivered and reached towards him.

'No, no, Lew! I didn't mean, I wasn't going to help him. I – I – '

'No?' sneered Grunfeld. 'Why do you think I came back if I didn't expect it? You won't fall for anyone else in a hurry, I'll see to that. I – '

'Lew! Forgive me – this once, just this once! I can't live four days without the snow, I tell you I can't!' She seemed to jump from the bed, was grovelling at his knees again. 'Just a little shot – a half, a quarter once a day, just a grain, that's all!'

He pushed her away contemptuously.

As he turned the key in the lock she rushed to the door and beat on it in a frenzy, but there was no answer beyond the hollow echo of her clenched fists on steel.

*   *   *

'Yes,' said Mannering, 'I *fell*, sergeant. Sorry to have given you people all this bother, but it will happen. I wasn't tight, either.'

The florid-faced sergeant at the Lambeth Police Station

looked at him dubiously.

'And I was in the water a long time, sergeant,' Mannering murmured gently. 'I got very cold. Another cup of cocoa, and I'll be your friend for life. And then if you'll lend me a spare coat and get me a cab, I'll stop worrying you.'

Ten minutes later Mannering alighted at his flat and was able to get upstairs without being observed. He tipped the man who had accompanied him, and sent the spare coat back with his compliments. Still mentally bemused, he ran a hot bath, and took a whisky-and-soda before getting into it. A brisk rub down, and half-an-hour's relaxation in an easy chair brought him nearer to normal, but there were moments when his ears began to throb, and he seemed to feel the beating of the water against his chest, the pressure on his lungs.

Slowly a clearer picture of what had happened emerged. Grunfeld – Legrand – Minx. All were indelibly printed on his mind, people he would never fail to recognise if he glimpsed them for an instant. He knew just how close to death he had been. Yet he was alive.

Reaching for the telephone he dialled a Mayfair number and asked for Lorna. She answered at once.

'John! How are you?'

'In abject need of moral support at the moment.'

'If you think I'm capable of giving it, I'll be round in a quarter-of-an-hour, darling.'

Mannering replaced the receiver with a smile, hesitated, and then dialled an Aldgate number. This time a man's voice, cultured and pleasing, answered him.

'Flick?'

'Mannering!'

'Yes,' said Mannering, 'and I'm going to worry you again, old man. Have you heard of the loss of the Louis stars?'

'From – Versailles? As a matter of fact I have. John, you weren't in that, were you? I thought –'

'I'm being dragged into it,' said Mannering briefly. 'Will you be at home in a couple of hours?'

'Can be. Don't forget that I, too, have officially retired.'

'With your ear to the ground,' chuckled Mannering. 'I'm coming with the best of motives, don't let your conscience be troubled.'

Mannering knew Leverson for one of the few men who vindicated the theory that there could be honour among thieves. He had never known Leverson try to trick or cheat

46

him – nor had anyone for that matter. Leverson handled his deals quickly, efficiently, and without undue haggling; while to the outside world he appeared to be a retired antique dealer and a somewhat prosy relic of the past.

The bell shrilled and Lorna came in, a chinchilla cape over her dark evening gown.

At sight of her Mannering felt a quick, comforting serenity.

He would probably not have been so had he seen the shadowed figure watching intently all those who left, or entered, his flat.

Lorna dropped her cape on to a chair and eyed Mannering with concern. Her smile disappeared.

'Trouble?'

'It could be, yes.'

Lorna nodded and waited. The expression in Mannering's eyes worried her. He seemed to be looking beyond her, as if he could see something she would not be able to understand.

'The name of the man who organised the Versailles robbery was Grunfeld,' said Mannering abruptly.

'Grunfeld – you know that? Already?'

'We might almost be called old acquaintances,' said Mannering. 'Not a nice acquaintance. Now the river patrol –'

Her hand tightened on his arm.

'What are you talking about?'

'The good souls who rescued me from the barge,' said Mannering, meditatively. 'They covered me in blankets and took me to Lambeth station, where I conferred and drank cocoa with a sergeant who didn't believe me. I *was* getting cold when they arrived, the cocoa was needed, and – sorry, darling! Let me work the mood off, it won't take long.'

Lorna said gently: 'Now supposing you start at the beginning.'

'The end is so much simpler, but if you want it that way –'

He had a graphic way of sketching events so that she could almost see them happening. He talked for twenty minutes, tersely, and to the point, and when he finished she was looking sombrely into his eyes.

Her first question was strictly common sense.

'Why didn't you tell Bristow right away? The whole crowd probably will be missing when the police get there.'

'It wouldn't have been any good,' said Mannering. 'From the little information I can give Bill he wouldn't find the place in a year. Don't make any mistake about the efficiency of Grunfeld and company. I – ' He stood up suddenly and stepped to the curtained window. 'Lorna, I can't help it and I know it's damned silly, but I'm more worried about this business than I've been about anything. I've met crooks both high and low, but Grunfeld and Legrand have a – what's the word? – a completeness I've seen nowhere else. Grunfeld may be English, but he has all the qualities of the worst kind of Prussian, and I needn't enlarge on that. The way he struck that girl –'

'And you think he's got Annette,' said Lorna slowly.

'I think it's more than possible.'

'Yet you haven't told Bristow,' she said dispassionately. 'Shall I ring him now?'

'I –' He shrugged. 'Well, yes, go ahead if you think it'll do any good – What's the matter?'

'Engaged.'

'Fate, you see.'

'I needn't stop trying.' She had replaced the receiver for a moment, and as she stretched out her hand to lift it again the telephone bell burred sharply: Mannering smiled.

'Evidently fate means us to get this call before breaking the news to Bristow. Who is it?'

'Leverson,' she said.

'Phew! Quick work.' He took the receiver from her. 'Hallo, Flick.'

Leverson's voice held a sharper expression than when the Baron had heard it half-an-hour before.

'John, you were serious just now?'

'I was, and am, very much so. Why?'

'Normally I don't touch anything when there's murder in the background,' said Flick, 'but I've had an offer of one of the stars – yes, it's the original and identical, you can be sure of that. Well?'

Mannering drew a deep breath and pushed his chair back.

'I'm coming over right away,' he said.

*　　*　　*

Detective-Sergeant Tanker Tring was not a brilliant policeman in any sense of the word. He was a gangling man with large, knuckly hands, and a bony, melancholy face in which doleful eyes held a suggestion of chronic complaint. He had been a sergeant when Bristow had joined the Force, and was likely to remain one.

But he was thorough.

As he waited outside Mannering's flat the memory of the

dozen occasions when the Baron had outwitted him afforded him ample material for gloomy reflection. Like Bristow, he could never bring himself to dislike Mannering, but also like Bristow he lived for the moment when he would hold the Baron on a charge which could not be evaded.

With a single-track mind he was now concentrating on the job in hand, excluding all others. Among them was a small man lounging a few yards along the street.

And then a cheerful voice broke across his thoughts.

'Hallo, Tanker, how's Mrs T, and all the little T's?'

Tanker swallowed.

'The Missus don't complain,' he muttered. He was always out of his depths with Mannering, who might, for all Tring knew, be planning a burglary under his very nose.

'Excellent woman,' said Mannering. 'No wonder you always look so happy, Tanker. How's the Yard, and old Bill?'

'*Mister* Bristow, sir, is A.1.'

'My love to him,' said Mannering. 'And a hint to you. That little fellow along the road has been loitering there for at least two hours. I don't like it.'

'*Two?*'

'To my knowledge,' said Mannering with a shrug.

He stepped off the pavement as a taxi cruised towards him, and jumped in, stating the single word '*Mendor's*' loudly enough for Tring to hear. Tring heard, made a mental note of it, and then looked sharply at the little man, who had jumped towards a Morris 8 parked nearby.

Tring could also move fast.

He reached the car as the man let in the clutch.

'*Here,*' he said, 'I want a word with you.'

The little man's foot left the clutch, although the engine was still humming, and he stared up into Tring's face. He did not recognise him as a sergeant, but 'police' was stamped indelibly on Tring's face and bearing.

The man forgot Mannering's cab, and his orders from Legrand to follow if Mannering appeared; he felt only fear.

He flung out a fist, caught Tring in the stomach, and started the Morris with a speed that shot him forward before Tring had recovered his balance.

Mannering, looking through the rear window of the cab and knowing he was not followed, smiled at a job well done.

Twenty minutes later he was approaching Flick Leverson's

three-storeyed house in Aldgate.

Leverson opened the door himself. He was nearly as tall as Mannering, but older by thirty years. His left coat-sleeve hung empty, a relic of the first World War.

'It's good to see you,' he said as they shook hands. 'But I'm not sure that I like this business, John.'

'I'm quite sure I don't,' said Mannering drily, as he followed Leverson to a large, low-ceilinged room in which a silver Genoese table reflected the flickering flames of a fire which Leverson usually kept burning winter and summer. There was an air of mellowness about that room which might have been expected in a country mansion. In Aldgate it was incongruous, yet to Mannering it seemed a fitting background for the fence.

'A little Couvoisier, I think,' said Leverson as Mannering sat down. 'Well, John – am I to have the full story?'

'It might be risky if you know too much,' Mannering replied, cupping his glass in his hand thoughtfully.

'Never mind that – how do you feel about it?'

'I'd like to talk, and I may need real help later. But before we go into it, are you sure you've had a genuine star offered you? There are' – he seemed to see Grunfeld's cold eyes appraising him – 'several good paste ones about, I'm told.'

Leverson smiled.

'No, this is a real one, John. Unless you can detect a flaw – '

And Mannering stared incredulously as the fence took a small case from his pocket, opened it, and held towards him a star-shaped diamond which glittered and scintillated a thousand fires, and seemed to promise a million more.

Chapter 9
More of Annette

Mannering eyed the star for fully twenty seconds. Leverson watched him without smiling: he knew that there was already blood on the diamond, and was afraid that one day Mannering would take a risk too many.

'Satisfied, John?'

'Yes. You're right, there's no doubt about it.'

Leverson shrugged.

'It came from someone who doesn't know me, on a recommendation from Paris as far as I can see.'

'Paris?' Mannering rubbed his chin thoughtfully. 'So there's another French angle, is there? Interesting. Just when did you get it?'

'Ten minutes before I phoned you, from a Frenchman who called himself Duval. He had a letter from Grionde, and Grionde is reliable enough, you know that. Does it help?'

'Not much, but Duval might, if I can get at him.'

Leverson pursed his lips.

'I doubt whether I'll ever see him again. I'm to send word to Grionde if I'm going to buy, and remit to Paris. If my answer's no, Grionde will send me instructions what to do with the star. Our man is careful, John.'

'Yes,' said Mannering, and his eyes were hard. 'If he's connected with some gentlemen I've recently met, that's understandable. This is going to be a vicious business, Flick, take my advice and keep just as clear of it as you can.'

'You're telling *me* to be careful?' Leverson chuckled. 'Do you want the star?'

'I want the police to have it.'

'I can't arrange that.'

'No. What price does Duval want for the single stone?'

'Ten thousand, less my commission. But if you're thinking of buying, we can waive that. Say eight thousand –'

'Say nothing,' said Mannering. 'There's no reason why you shouldn't make money even if you are on the retired list. Have it looked after for me, Flick – no, on second thoughts,

I'll take it with me, and I'll send a cheque round in the morning. It isn't likely you'll get any of the others offered, but I'll take whatever I can, and get my money back afterwards – if I'm lucky.'

'Odd fish, aren't you?' Leverson said.

'Odd? Not really. The motive's shifted, that's all. I want – well, in this particular case I want to have another meeting with a Mr Louis Grunfeld. Does the name mean anything to you?'

'No.'

'Legrand?'

Leverson frowned.

'Legrand – I've heard that somewhere, it has a Paris connection, too. I'll ask Grionde to tell me what he knows, and get a description of the man I've got in mind. Be careful, John.'

Mannering rested a hand for a moment on Leverson's shoulder.

'If it's to be my funeral, let's keep it that way. Remember you're taking no further interest in this, Flick, and keep your enquiries very much to yourself. If Grunfeld thought you were involved, it might prove to be a very poor show for you indeed. Clear?'

'Very,' said Leverson drily. 'All right, give me a ring if there's anything else you want.'

Mannering left the fence's house a few minutes afterwards and walked sharply towards Aldgate High Street. He had not fully recovered from the surprise of seeing the star in Leverson's hand, and he was hoping that there would be a way of tracing the man Duval. That Duval was a member of, or agent for, the gang who had put paste stones in Vincenne's brief-case appeared a reasonable possibility; and Grunfeld would also be looking for him.

An odd set-up altogether.

Mannering hired a cab from Aldgate Station, directing the man to take him to Scotland Yard. Now that he was recovering from the ordeal of the earlier evening he found his thoughts turning more and more towards Annette. He had disliked the fear in her voice when she had telephoned, and he was convinced that she had asked him to forget her because she had been ordered to do so. But by whom?

Grunfeld was the obvious possibility, but Mannering did not think it by any means certain. He could not keep the memory of Annette's despairing face from his mind, time and time again he told himself that she had been acting. But he was convinced that there had been no histrionics when she had learned of the death of her father. That news had been a shock.

Yet within three minutes she had calmly called a cab.

Big Ben struck half-past eleven as Mannering paid his man off and turned towards the gates of Scotland Yard. The irony of entering Scotland Yard with a star in his pocket made him smile. There was a modicum of risk in it, but he did not consider it enough to worry about.

Bristow, he found, was not in, but Lynch was still in his office.

He did not look up from the papers he was studying until Mannering had selected a chair and leaned back in it comfortably.

Then he said: 'Mannering, one of these days you'll take too much for granted. I've got several things to ask you, but the most important is about your swim tonight. Since when have you started feeling giddy on the Embankment?'

Mannering raised his eyebrows.

'You can give me advice, but you can't tell me what to do,' he said lightly. 'I'd hoped that was quite clear by now. I assure you, however, that I was not looking for trouble just then.'

'But you got it.'

'As Bristow says, it always comes while I'm about. Lynch –' Mannering's eyes gleamed, and the Superintendent wondered uneasily what new trick was about to be played on him. 'I've good news for you.'

'I'll be grateful to hear it.'

'You don't sound grateful. Listen. I was held up in my own flat, kidnapped – yes, *kidnapped* – and between ourselves I'm lucky to be here. I had an offer of joining forces with a Mr Grunfeld, and a Mr Legrand – forces operating against the police, Lynch, so of course I refused –'

He broke off deliberately. Lynch was frowning, trying to conceal the depth of his interest but failing to do so. He tapped lightly but impatiently on his desk.

'Don't hold it.'

'Dramatic pause,' smiled Mannering. 'It's all true, you know. I refused, and I was put aside for an interview with the river. Object – drowning. I had other ideas, and incredible good luck. Lynch, what would your sergeant have thought

54

had he known I'd just taken one of the stars from the safe of a very bad man?'

'*What?* You –'

Lynch jerked upright.

Mannering slipped his hand into his pocket and brought out the case. He tossed it carelessly to the policeman and sat back to savour the moment thoroughly. He saw the incredulity on Lynch's face as the case was opened.

'Where'd you get it?'

'That's the trouble, I don't know – exactly.'

He related what had happened truthfully enough – up to a point. From then onwards he gave a fictitious account of finding a safe with the keys handy, and from it extracting the stone. When he had finished Lynch lifted a telephone and spent five minutes giving instructions to the River Police. That done, he turned to Mannering.

'Can you describe Grunfeld and Legrand?'

Mannering did so with graphic realism.

'A couple of gentlemen I am not likely to forget,' he added grimly.

'You should have reported this the moment you were free, not left it until now,' Lynch said accusingly. 'You dodged Tring an hour or so ago – why?'

'Dodged?' repeated Mannering. He was not smiling now, and his eyes were hard and equally accusing. 'Lynch, I came here to put a trump card on the table. You've got it, but I'll keep the next one up my sleeve if Tring continues to pester me. Grunfeld's your man, and I've told you that he admitted the murder of Vincenne.'

'Yes,' said Lynch, slowly. 'All right, Mannering, I'll talk to the A.C. in the morning.'

Lynch did not continue, for his door opened abruptly, with only the lightest of knocks, and Bristow, his steps quickened by excitement, entered.

'Superintendent, I – *Mannering!*'

'Go on,' said Lynch.

Bristow pulled at his moustache.

'I – the Vincenne girl,' he said, and Mannering felt his pulse quicken as he waited for the policeman's words. Lynch, too, had grown tense, although his face was expressionless. 'She's been picked up in a boarding-house in Streatham, and they're bringing her right over.'

* * *

Annette had been detained for questioning.

She was also in a raging temper, her blue eyes flashing, her small hands clenched.

'Why, why, why?' she demanded. 'Why do you catch me when you look for the murderer of my father? Answer me! I am a citizen of France, am I not, and demand to see my Consul!'

Lynch nodded comprehendingly, soothingly.

'Of course, Miss Vincenne, if there is any need for you to complain I shall expect you to do so. All I want is a few questions answered, and then you will be quite free to go where you like.' He turned his head. 'Do you mind leaving us, Mannering?'

Mannering moved to the door, ready for an outburst from Annette at the mention of his name. He saw her body stiffen; then she turned rigidly to Lynch.

'The questions – what are they?'

Mannering went outside with his mind in a whirl. Acting again; she was always acting. But it seemed incredible that she had deliberately avoided doing anything which would show the police she knew him, for she could not know how much he had told them.

He walked slowly towards the main hall of the Yard.

He had what amounted to Lynch's conditional under-taking to let him have a reasonably free hand, although he knew that this might not be condoned by Ffoulkes. Yet it seemed that for the first time in the life of the Baron, there was a prospect of working without fear of the police at his heels.

It would certainly make it easier for him to cope with Grunfeld; but it was Annette's attitude which loomed largest in his thoughts. First at Portland Place, then on the telephone, now here; she contrived to puzzle and perturb him, to earn at once his sympathy and distrust.

'*Where is she?*'

A voice from the entrance hall startled him. It was high-pitched and angry. Mannering hurried forward in time to see a youngster of rather more than medium height, fair-haired and well-dressed, glaring at the sergeant on duty.

The sergeant's voice – quiet and placatory – answered him.

'She won't be long, sir, Superintendent Lynch is just having a few words with her.'

Mannering's interest quickened.

'Don't lie to me!' The tone was that of a well-educated

56

Englishman of good social standing. The face was not particularly handsome, although even flushed with anger it had attraction, and the jaw suggested stubbornness. 'You've gone a lot too far –'

Mannering paused, a yard or so away.

'Worried about Miss Vincenne?' he asked helpfully.

The youth glared.

'What the devil do *you* know about her?'

'Only that I've just left her with Superintendent Lynch, who doesn't expect to be free for half-an-hour.'

'I'm staying right here,' snapped the youngster truculently.

Mannering shrugged.

'You must please yourself, of course, but you'll only waste time and temper if you stay. I was' – he went on quietly – 'an acquaintance of her father's.'

'Of old Raoul? I – *what* was your name?'

'Mannering.'

'*Mannering!* You – ' The youngster drew a sharp breath, and for a moment Mannering could not understand his expression. Then sharply: 'I'd like a word with you. When Miss Vincenne's free, sergeant, ask her to wait for me here. Clayton's the name.'

'I'll see to it, sir.'

Following Mannering, Clayton said nothing until they reached the pavement in Parliament Street. He stepped towards a low-hung Frazer Nash, and paused.

'Know anywhere handy?'

'There's a quiet place near Victoria Street, not five minutes away.'

'Hop in,' said Clayton curtly.

Mannering obeyed, knowing that he was taking a chance. Clayton might be what he made out – a friend of Annette's. On the other hand he could be one of the people who had frightened her.

It was a gamble worth taking.

Mannering gave directions, and four minutes later Clayton stopped the car outside a small restaurant just off Victoria Street. Not until they were seated at a secluded table did he speak again.

Clayton, Mannering decided, was either damnably worried or in a furious temper; probably a little of both.

'Look here, Mannering,' he said at last, 'what have you been doing to Annette?'

'Little but offer advice,' answered Mannering quietly.

'Oh, don't try to put me off like that!'

Mannering said: 'What right have you to know?'

'I'm engaged to her.'

'Is that official?'

'Well, sort of.'

Clayton looked sulky as he contemplated an unpalatable fact. It was plain enough that he was in love with Annette, not so plain what she felt for him.

Mannering had ordered coffee, and was silent as a waiter brought it.

'Now try to get a hold of yourself, Clayton. I gave Miss Vincenne a nasty shock this afternoon, but someone had to. Did you know her father well?'

The colour drained from Clayton's cheeks.

'*Did* I know him?'

'Just that,' said Mannering. 'He was killed in a street accident.'

The young man's lips worked, his eyes set in an alarm that seemed unnatural. With him, just as with Annette and her father, there was an impression of acting, as though *something* was false or forced. Was it merely a *penchant* for histrionics, or had it a more serious foundation?

Clayton gasped out: 'But it *can't* be! I've backed him with my last penny, I haven't a *sou* left. I – '

He stopped, and turned his face away, while Mannering seemed to hear Vincenne's voice convincing this youngster of the justice of his claims to the fortunes of Louis Quinze. He could imagine the tragedy that faced young Clayton.

And Annette.

Chapter 10
Clayton's Story

Mannering did not speak for several minutes, and then he said casually:

'How much did you know about the stars, Clayton?'

The youngster started.

'Stars? What stars?'

Mannering's voice hardened.

'You'll find me a *little* more sympathetic than the police, Clayton. Cells aren't comfortable places, you know.'

Clayton swore.

'The police can go to the devil, you can't scare me like that. They were his, weren't they? The old man wasn't a fool. The *stars* were his.'

Could the youngster really believe such a story?

'You may think so, but the *Sûreté* certainly does not,' Mannering said sharply. 'I may be able to help you, but when Lynch learns you followed Annette he'll want to know why.'

'But I didn't steal the damned things!'

'So I gathered. Nevertheless you know something about it. Just how much?'

'I don't see any reason why I should confide in you,' said Clayton defiantly. 'Who are you, anyway?'

Mannering shrugged.

'All right. The question is, do you or don't you want to help Annette?'

Clayton clenched his fist above the table.

'What do you want to know? I tell you, if they hurt that kid – '

'Don't talk like a fool,' said Mannering, 'the police won't hurt her, although others might and she could easily be safer at Cannon Row than with you. I want to know your story, where it concerns Annette, her father, and the stars of Louis.'

Clayton muttered sulkily: 'There isn't much to it. Old Raoul was staying at my place a few months ago, and got talking about being a direct descendant of Louis Quinze, and wanting money to fight for some of the Louis gems. Annette seemed keen, so I – I put up five thousand, all my capital, for legal expenses. Most of it was spent in a few months, and we weren't any further ahead, and then Vincenne said he was making arrangements to get hold of some of the jewels to pay the extra expenses and give me a bit back. I – I didn't realise what he meant at first, and before I did the job was done. Anyhow, they *were* his.' Clayton glared, still defiant. 'I wasn't going to let him down then.'

'No,' said Mannering.

It seemed a convincing enough story, and it was easy to believe that Clayton, at first sceptical, had seen and loved Annette, and soon been persuaded.

'Well, what else do you want?' demanded Clayton. 'Old Raoul said he had found a buyer for them, but he didn't talk much. I know he flew to and from Paris. When he hadn't turned up at the Regal Annette said she was going to see you, and insisted on going alone.'

'How did she know he wasn't at the Regal?'

'We were both waiting nearby for him. I – here, Mannering! He had those things with him – *God!* Did the police – ' He gasped the words, and half-rose from his seat.

'They didn't find them on him,' said Mannering, and the alarm in the youngster's face died down. 'But they do know he had them once. That's why they're interested in Annette. No, don't start flying off the handle again. Did Vincenne take the stars himself?'

For the first time Clayton's expression relaxed.

'Don't be a lunatic, man, of course he didn't, he wouldn't have had the nerve. He got in touch with a fellow named Grunfeld, or something like that, and they were going to split fifty-fifty.'

'Have you ever seen this Grunfeld?'

'Good Lord, no!'

'You needn't be sorry about that,' said Mannering, and glanced at his watch. 'We'd better be getting along if you want to take Annette away. And if she does get permission to leave the Yard I'll want to talk to her.'

'She can decide about that herself.'

'We'll see,' said Mannering shortly.

They reached the Yard a few minutes before Annette came in sight with Lynch at her side.

'I've told you,' Lynch was saying heavily, 'that you must stay within call, Miss Vincenne, in case we want you again. It will be extremely foolish of you to move from your present address without advising us. Goodnight.'

Annette looked at him scornfully. She saw Mannering, but ignored him. She could not ignore Clayton, for he strode up to her, and gripped her arm.

'Darling, did they – '

'Take me away!' she said sharply. 'They tried to tell me that my father stole the stars of Louis. Would a man steal from himself?'

Mannering nodded to Lynch, and followed the couple. He must find out where Annette had been when she phoned him, and why she had changed her attitude so suddenly. Annette walked straight to the Frazer Nash. Mannering put a hand on the door next to her and said:

'Annette, isn't it time you told someone the truth?'

She did not look at him, but kept her eyes on the road ahead. Her voice held an undercurrent of passion that could not be mistaken.

'Do you want me killed, too? Isn't one enough for you? If my father had never known you he would still be alive. *You* killed him, *you*!'

The accusation was so unexpected, so vehement, that Mannering could find no words, could only stand and stare at her set profile, before Clayton let in the clutch and the car moved slowly away.

* * *

'It could be,' Mannering said, 'that she believed it.'

Lorna brushed back a lock of hair, as she leaned against the cushions of a divan at her Chelsea studio. Beneath the ceiling-window her easel stood, supporting a half-finished portrait. About the walls stood other partly-furnished or experimental canvasses, all showing an originality of touch that demanded the attention if not approval of the critics.

'Yes,' she admitted, 'it is possible. It must have been a startling revelation to a man with a Robin Hood complex.'

'So startling that if Lynch had asked me just then if I were the Baron I would probably have said yes. I've never been so shocked in my life.'

'You'll recover. And now let's be serious.'

'Not *all* the time,' pleaded Mannering. 'From the moment that Grunfeld knows I'm alive there's going to be time for sobriety; we may as well laugh while we can. Lorna – '

'Hm-hm?'

'London isn't just the place for you at the moment, is it? So many cooler spots, and – '

'You're afraid Grunfeld might retaliate through me?'

'All right, I am.' Mannering's face was suddenly hard. 'I'll tell you. Grunfeld will stop precisely at nothing, sweetheart, and I don't want the worry of you on my mind as well as the rest of the business.'

'Couldn't you give up the rest of the business?'

'Not with Legrand about,' Mannering said. 'And there's Minx, too.' He stood up quickly, took her hands and pulled her towards him. 'Slip down to Hampshire for a week or two, Lorna, your mother's going today, I know.'

Lorna frowned.

'Only if you promise faithfully to send for me if I can be the slightest help.'

'Done!' said Mannering. 'Lorna, I – *blast* that telephone!'

It rang insistently, and Lorna answered it after a short interval, only to hold it towards him.

'Whoever it is, confound him,' said Mannering.

'Flick I think.'

'Remark withdrawn . . . Hallo – yes, Flick?'

Leverson's voice came clearly over the telephone. There was urgency in it.

'I haven't much time,' Leverson said tersely. 'Two things, John. I've talked with Grionde, and he recognises Legrand. The man's wanted in Paris for two knife murders. A killer, pure and simple.'

'I'd gathered that,' Mannering said grimly.

'All right, but he's quite ruthless. Now the other thing – Grionde assures me that Duval would not normally associate with Legrand, and doubts very much whether they're connected in this business except through a go-between. Does that fit in?'

'The mysterious second party – yes.'

'Good. And John – Duval's coming to collect his money this morning after all, at twelve-thirty. If you want to see him – '

'See him!' snapped the Baron. 'I want a lot more than that. Thanks, Flick, I'll be at hand and I'll follow him. That the lot?'

'Yes – and remember Legrand's reputation.'

'I'm not likely to forget,' said Mannering. He replaced the

telephone, and his eyes were glinting when he looked at Lorna. The moment for *tendresse* had passed, and she could see the Baron there, not Mannering. 'Action, darling. You start for Hampshire this afternoon, if you can, and I'll phone you this evening. The make-up set, now –'

'Is it going to be safe?'

'I don't want Duval to recognise me as Mannering,' said Mannering, 'so I'll operate as Mr Jonathan Moore for an hour or two.'

From the cupboards beneath the paint cabinet he took a fully-equipped theatrical make-up box. Stripping off his coat and shirt he set to work with a quick, deliberate sureness of touch, gradually obliterating one face, bringing to life another, a somewhat florid, plump, middle-aged countenance, the mouth turning down with a constant grievance. Finished at last, he peered appraisingly at himself in the mirror.

'How's the time, darling?'

'Ten to twelve.'

'Ring for a taxi, will you?'

She moved to the telephone, while he worked a thin rubber covering over his strong white teeth, making them look discoloured as if with nicotine and imperfect cleaning.

'All done, but for the wardrobe,' Mannering smiled as Lorna returned from the telephone. 'I'll be out in five minutes, angel, and then I'll be off.'

From a wardrobe Lorna handed him a suit, a little too shapely, made by an East End tailor, and Mannering dressed in it quickly. It was all that was wanted to make the illusion perfect, and Lorna laughed when she saw him.

'Does Mr Moore get a farewell kiss?'

'Idiot.' As she came close he saw that her eyes were troubled, and he felt the tenseness of her body. 'John, be careful. You've rather frightened me with Grunfeld.'

'Not as much as I'm going to frighten him,' Mannering said easily. 'Hampshire this afternoon, remember.'

'Yes, I'll go.'

'Fine,' said Mannering. 'There's one other thing. There's a Rutland family of Claytons; it's just possible that Annette's Clayton is one of them. If you could find out whether there's a Richard in the family, and get a rough description, it might help.'

Three minutes later Mannering leapt into a waiting cab.

The mid-day traffic in the West End and the City was thick,

but at twenty-five minutes past twelve Mannering was stepping towards Wine Street. Duval, he knew, might be early for the appointment with Leverson, but the fence would contrive to keep him there until some minutes past the half-hour.

Mannering strolled past Flick's house. In less than two minutes the front door opened, and a man stepped into the street.

He was a tall man, dressed in a dark suit, a white muffler knotted at the throat. A hat was pulled low over his forehead, but could not entirely hide the sharp, restless movement of his eyes. Yet the thing which would print Duval indelibly on Mannering's mind was a scar running almost from ear to lips on the left side of his face. It was ugly, yet Duval looked neither villainous nor repugnant.

Duval hesitated, and then turned towards Aldgate. Mannering had been walking in the same direction, and it was not difficult to follow the Frenchman who had eight thousand pounds of Mannering's money – payment for the star – in his pocket.

Duval threaded his way through the crowds of hawkers and fruit vendors without difficulty or hesitation. Mannering followed on the other side of the road. Duval's height made him easy enough to pick out, and Mannering did not feel that there was much chance of losing him. But he was puzzled, for Duval gave the impression that he knew exactly where he was going.

Certainly he had trodden this part of London before. He went down the short cobbled stretch of Tower Hill towards the Tower itself, as a cargo-steamer went sluggishly by on the river. Tower Bridge was up, its two halves yawning like a giant excavator, and there were long lines of traffic on either side.

Duval went into the Tower grounds, walking at the same sharp pace towards one of the old guns pointing towards the south bank. Almost opposite the drawbridge and gates of the Bloody Tower, he stopped.

Mannering sat down abruptly on a seat with one space vacant. He felt his pulse beating fast, for he needed no telling that Duval had a rendezvous here with someone who, in all likelihood, would claim a share of the proceeds from the star, and perhaps had the other four.

A clock struck one.

Duval had been waiting for ten minutes; now he looked

impatiently about him, his eyes searching the strolling crowds.

Straight to Duval walked a well-dressed man of medium height, remarkable only because of the contrast he presented to the indifferent dress of the crowd about him. He was bareheaded, and wore a carnation in his right lapel.

Twice he fingered his buttonhole.

They reached each other.

There was a brief conversation which Mannering could not hear, and then Duval put his hand into his breast pocket and drew out a packet a little larger than a wallet. He held it for a moment as though reluctant to let go, and for the first time Mannering heard what he said:

'For me, *M'sieu*, first please.'

The other scowled and shrugged, drew out a wallet and from it took an envelope. Envelope and packet changed hands simultaneously.

Deeply interested, Mannering failed to see the cat-like approach of a small man appearing as if from nowhere. Only when he turned his head did Mannering catch a glimpse of the face. It was one he would never forget – for it was Legrand's.

Mannering stood up abruptly, but he was too late to stop what happened. Legrand, moving swiftly, reached Duval and the other, and snatched at the thicker packet. The well-dressed man uttered a sharp exclamation, and his right hand dropped towards his pocket – the gunman's instinctive movement, Mannering knew. But Legrand hit both him and Duval full in the stomach. Both men doubled up, but before they had recovered Legrand had melted into the crowd.

Not entirely, for Mannering had contrived, in apparent innocence, to be standing in his way.

A dozen or so bystanders were now clustered round the assaulted men as the tall figure of a policeman approached. Mannering was within a yard of Legrand and close to his right hand, which still clutched the packet.

In that split-second Mannering acted.

He snatched the packet away and at the same time kicked his ankle. As the gunman recovered himself Mannering slipped back into the crowd and out of sight. Delighted, he doubled back to Duval and the stranger, the packet safely in his pocket.

He pressed forward to make sure that he did not lose sight of Duval's companion, his satisfaction at the success of his own manoeuvre suddenly shot by doubt.

How had Legrand known of Duval, and the rendezvous?

Chapter 11
Home of Matthew Garston

The well-dressed man, with some reluctance, gave his name as Matthew Garston. With that, and the assurance that nothing had been stolen, the policeman appeared to be content.

Quickly the crowd melted away, and with it, Duval. Doggedly, Mannering followed Garston, keeping at a safe distance. Heading for the Minories, Garston did not once look round.

Mannering, prepared for any emergency, heard a taxi rattling over the cobbles behind him, and lifted a hand. It was as well he took the precaution, for halfway up the Minories Garston stepped up to a black Wolseley 16, opened the door savagely and slammed it behind him.

Mannering opened the partition.

'Let that Wolseley get in front, driver, and then follow it. Understand?'

A long ride through the City and West End followed.

At Putney Bridge Garston turned right along the Lower Richmond Road, and in that district Mannering knew that he was going to have trouble in following him with the cab. The traffic was no longer thick enough to enable the driver to remain unnoticed.

The Wolseley stopped outside a tobacconist's, and Garston went inside. Mannering slipped from his cab, paid his cabby handsomely, and walked quickly to a nearby garage with a 'taxi' sign displayed. Keeping an eye on the tobacconist's, he negotiated with an alert-eyed youngster for an old Armstrong-Siddeley fitted with a taxi-meter.

'Just get my hat, sir, won't be – '

'Never mind your hat. When that Wolseley starts, follow it.'

The youngster stared through the glass partition.

'Follow *that* car, sir? I expect Mr Garston will be garaging it in a few minutes. He only lives just round the corner.'

The words were like a blow in the face to Mannering; in that moment he had aroused the youth's suspicions, a youth who in all likelihood would not hesitate to tell a customer that someone was interested in him.

He needed to gain time.

'Mr Garston's a good customer?'

'He's regular, sir.' Something in the other's manner made Mannering suspect that Garston was not popular, and a way out seemed to present itself.

'I see. Can I trust you to keep silent?'

'Yes, sir.'

Mannering parted with a ten-shilling note, and the youngster grinned, touching his forehead.

'You won't want the cab now, sir?'

'Oh, yes, you can drive me past Mr Garston's house, and then on to Piccadilly.'

A right turn and then a left led to Steen Way, a short cul-de-sac in which stood seven big, detached houses.

'Number 4, sir – the name's Leeminx.'

Immediately Mannering's mind flew to the woman who had crouched in front of Grunfeld, the woman in terror because she had been threatened with the withdrawal of her supply of cocaine.

He said with an effort: 'Rather a large house, isn't it? Or has Mr Garston a family?'

'Not that he shouts about,' said the youth with a grin. 'Lives there with two servants, two guys I wouldn't like to meet in a dark alley.'

'Ah well, that is all I want to see, just now. On the other side of Putney Bridge I will come in the front with you.'

'Right, sir.'

A hundred yards from Leeminx they passed Garston carrying a small brown-paper package, larger than the one Mannering had in his pocket, and tied about with white string.

When he changed from the tonneau to the seat next to the driver he said casually:

'Mr Garston buys all his cigarettes from that shop?'

'Well, I suppose so,' said the lad, 'it's his own, so he ought to.'

'Oh? A tobacconist, is he?'

'Yes, sir, got four or five shops I believe, and seems to do pretty well out of them. Don't have his name over the top, though, calls them the Cigar Stores.'

'I see.'

Mannering was thoughtful, thinking chiefly of the prospect of a visit to Leeminx that night. It was possible, of course, that it was wired. He would try to get inside by day, if only to examine the fittings at the windows and doors. Only in emergency would he try to force entry into premises he did not know well.

He considered what kind of explanation he should give the youngster at his side to cover his interest in the house.

'So,' he mused aloud, 'Mr Garston is quite a well-to-do man? *You* would know whether he – er – settles his account in satisfactory fashion, wouldn't you?'

'Oh, yes, his money's all right,' said the youngster. 'He's not trying to bilk you, is he?'

'He put up a business proposition which did not entirely satisfy me,' said Mannering. 'A complete stranger to me, you see, and I like to make *personal* enquiries about my business associates. However, it is obvious that I need have no fears where Mr Garston is concerned.'

He left the subject, reasonably assured that the boy's curiosity was satisfied, and asked to be put down at Hyde Park.

The other drove off, and Mannering stood hesitating. To go to his own flat as Mr Moore might bring complications, and the same risk applied to the studio.

A service flat was the best solution.

Not for the first time he walked to Fuller Mansions, a block of flats in Park Lane, and took a two-roomed furnished apartment on the third floor. He paid cash for the first month's rent, and took immediate possession. The first thing he did was to examine the packet, finding eight bundles of twenty fifty-pound Bank of England notes; the second was to clean off the disguise. Twenty minutes later his face was John Mannering's, though his suit was Mr Moore's.

From his pocket he took a small, rolled mackintosh which reached to his knees, donned it, and hurried to his Brook Street flat. As he closed the door the telephone rang sharply.

He lifted it.

'Hallo, yes?'

'So you're there, are you?' grunted Bristow. 'I've been trying to get you all the morning. Sir David's at lunch now, but he wants to see you at three o'clock. I shouldn't be late, if I were you.'

'It sounds unpleasantly like an ultimatum,' said Mannering. 'Please tell the Assistant Commissioner that I shall be delighted to see him here at three o'clock, but the earliest I can get to the Yard is half-past five. Clear?'

'Mannering, I – '

'Just tell him that,' said Mannering, and rang off.

He frowned as he stepped into his bedroom. He had expected the call, and to antagonise the police was the last thing he wanted to do; but to submit to arbitrary orders would do more harm than good. He shrugged, bathed and changed into clothes that fitted him, and rang for a waiter. He ordered lunch with care, added a half bottle of Moselle, and mixed himself a weak whisky-and-soda as he waited for it. The first course had arrived, and he was sitting down when the telephone rang again.

Mannering scowled and lifted it, prepared for trouble from Bristow or Lynch.

'Who is that?'

'So you *are* there.' It was Grunfeld's voice.

'Certainly I'm here,' said Mannering, and laughed, knowing that laughter would infuriate Grunfeld. 'Very much so. Interesting little wad of bank-notes I collected this morning. Legrand nearly put them into my hand, I couldn't refuse.'

He heard Grunfeld gasp, knew the man was shaken.

'How the devil did you – '

'Come, come,' said Mannering, 'you really shouldn't get so heated – but thanks for calling.'

He heard the receiver bang down at the other end, and he could imagine Grunfeld's square, teutonic face flushed with anger, the furious glitter in his light blue eyes. He shrugged; an angry man was more liable to make mistakes than one who kept an even temper.

But Legrand would not easily get angry.

It was twenty-five to three when Mannering finished his lunch, and at twenty-to, Lorna rang through.

'I haven't much time, John, but I've learned a little about Clayton.'

'Good work.'

'You were right about him, he *is* one of the Rutland family. Apparently Richard recently inherited something like six thousand pounds from an uncle, and the Claytons are afraid he'll run through the inheritance before he can turn round.'

'He's done that all right,' said Mannering grimly. 'Where was he staying in London?'

'At the Junior Carlton until a few weeks ago, but he's not been heard of since – '

'Is this just gossip, darling, or is it reasonably sure?'

'Oh, it's sure enough. He still calls at the Junior Carlton for letters, but they either don't know, or won't, give his address.'

Lorna chatted on for a few minutes, and then rang off.

Mannering put down the receiver thoughtfully, thinking over Clayton's probably unwilling part in the robbery, and confirming his opinion that he would be the type to go through with any project once he had his teeth into it.

Then he pushed thought of the youngster aside, and pondered his own relationship with the police in this affair.

Would Ffoulkes swallow his pride and come?

The front door bell rang.

Mannering hesitated, and then stepped to a bureau in his bedroom, took an automatic from it and slipped it in his pocket. He kept his left hand about it as he opened the door, for this might be Legrand, or one of Grunfeld's men, and not Ffoulkes.

Instead it was the last man Mannering expected to see, for it was *Clayton* –

A Clayton who looked as angry and worked up as he had been on the previous night.

Chapter 12
Legrand Tries Again

With the possibility of Ffoulkes arriving at any moment, Mannering had no desire at all to talk with Annette's *fiancé*. The youth was liable to blurt out things that could well incriminate Annette, and until Mannering knew the whole truth he did not want that. Despite his death or perhaps because of it, it was old Raoul, with the soft, urgent voice, and the appealing eyes, who mattered most of the trio. But Annette needed help.

'Where's Annette?'

The question jolted Mannering, as Clayton pushed his way through the door, and stood truculently in the middle of the hallway.

'Let me tell you, Mannering, I'm going to get at the truth. I wouldn't be surprised if you don't know a sight more about this business than you've pretended.'

Through the open door Mannering heard the lift going down. It might not be his man, but the chance of it being Ffoulkes was too great to risk. He had to act swiftly.

'If you want to talk, come in here,' he said, and he gripped Clayton's arm, leading him through the living-room into his own bedroom. 'Don't argue!' Clayton had started to open his lips, but closed them abruptly, momentarily startled by the urgency in Mannering's voice.

With cool precision Mannering hit Clayton sharply and scientifically, then hurried to the bureau from which he had taken the gun. In a false bottom controlled by a spring he had a chloroform pad. This he pressed over Clayton's mouth and nose, and watched him sink more deeply into unconsciousness.

The front door bell rang.

Mannering snatched the cord from his dressing-gown and tied it about Clayton's wrists, and ankles. He was breathing hard as he hurried across the room, straightening his coat as he went. The bell rang more insistently as he reached the hall, and a moment later he opened it to Ffoulkes and Bristow.

'Hallo, David, you're on time. Come in.' He smiled easily

and affably, motioning to chairs, and they sat down without speaking. Their manner was disturbing, although Mannering forced himself not to admit it. 'Coffee?'

'No, thanks.'

'Mannering – ' Ffoulkes ignored the proffered cigarette case, and his face was set and hostile. 'You've made a lot of capital out of the fact that you've been helping us.' He paused, and then went on: 'Lynch has reported what happened last night – *everything* that happened.'

Mannering tapped a cigarette on his thumb nail.

'You're not going to try to make capital out of that, I hope? For if the Press got the full story of how you regained one of the stars, so many pleasant things said about the police might be withdrawn. Don't,' went on Mannering with a disarming smile, 'misunderstand me. The last thing I want to do is to publish the story, it will come out only if my hand is forced.'

'Leave that for now,' said Ffoulkes. 'The point of interest is your connection with Annette Vincenne. Where is she?'

Mannering's tension grew.

'Should I know?'

'I wouldn't be surprised,' Ffoulkes said, heavily. 'She disappeared from her hotel this morning.'

'Disappeared? Or just went out?'

'There are signs that she left against her will. And – she had been chloroformed.'

Mannering's head jerked up.

'As the Baron uses chloroform we were rather interested,' said Ffoulkes evenly. 'If you had nothing to do with her disappearance, Mannering, perhaps you'll tell us where you have been.'

Ffoulkes's eyes did not leave Mannering's face. It was a bad moment, a dangerous one, for it was impossible to prove that he had not been near the Streatham hotel in which the girl had stayed. For a moment he felt the rising of panic; and then it eased, for neither could they prove that he had seen Annette.

'Just what time,' he demanded, 'would you like me to account for my movements?'

'Until half-past eleven.'

Relief filled Mannering.

'Here until ten o'clock, David, and the porter downstairs will confirm that. Chelsea until mid-day, at Miss Fauntley's studio. Just after eleven a frisky exchange with her char over

72

the weather. You know,' Mannering added gently, 'Lynch should have had her watched if she's so important.'

'He did,' said Ffoulkes. 'It appears our man was knocked down by a taxi outside the hotel.'

Mannering stiffened.

'That game again?'

Ffoulkes relaxed, and stretched his hand forward as if satisfied that he had heard the truth.

'I'll have that cigarette, John. Thanks. Now, quite seriously, what do you know about Annette Vincenne?'

'Precious little,' said Mannering. 'She knew her father was coming to see me, but she says she didn't know what it was about. I suppose it's natural she should associate me with his death; certainly she more than hinted that last night.'

'Hmm. Well now, this man Clayton. He reported that the girl was missing, and in a somewhat tempestuous manner. What do you know about him?'

'Personally, less than about Annette,' said Mannering, and he glanced at his watch. The chloroform should keep Clayton quiet for half-an-hour, but nearly fifteen minutes had gone, and some people were bad subjects. Within five minutes he must make an excuse for slipping into the bedroom.

There was no reason why he should hesitate to pass on such family history as he had gathered about Clayton, for Ffoulkes would not be long in obtaining the information Lorna had secured. He gave the essentials, and when he had finished, Ffoulkes nodded.

'It sounds reasonable.'

'And Grunfeld?' Mannering asked. 'Has Lynch told you of Grunfeld?'

'He has. Now let us get this quite clear – if the Baron shows himself, *you're* for it. This time I'll find a charge on which to hold you, and there'll be no getting away.' Ffoulkes stood up, his eyes hard. 'Is that fully understood?'

Mannering said: 'I told Lynch last night that Grunfeld is quite enough to handle at a time, and – ' He shrugged. 'I also told him that if he persisted in putting flatfoots around me, I might get obstreperous. It takes two to make a bargain.'

'I'll bear that in mind,' said Ffoulkes drily. 'All right, Bristow, I'll leave you to get a fuller statement about Grunfeld's place at Lambeth.' He nodded to Bristow, and stepped towards the door. 'I'll let myself out.'

He reached the hall door.

He opened it a little, stopped, and turned round.

'I want to know immediately if you hear anything from Clayton or the girl.'

'Leave it to me,' said Mannering. 'I – *God*!'

The exclamation seemed wrung from him.

For a moment both Mannering and Bristow stood motionless, staring towards Ffoulkes as the Assistant Commissioner threw up his hands with a sharp cry of pain.

They *saw* the blood on Ffoulkes's temple.

And then Mannering leapt towards the open door, while down the stairs of the block of flats a man rushed pell-mell.

*   *   *

Mannering raced along the passage to the stairs, the smell of the shot strong in his nostrils. He saw the lift standing empty where Ffoulkes and Bristow had left it, and jumped in, arriving at the ground floor twenty feet behind his quarry.

The gunman was nearing the front entrance and moving fast. Mannering snatched his automatic from his pocket, would have used it then but for the three people who turned suddenly into the flats. The gunman thudded into them and went sprawling.

He was up in a flash, his gun levelled.

Mannering swayed desperately to one side, as a bullet flashed past him. Running footsteps thudded across the pavement and the door of a waiting Morris 8 was torn open.

A hundred people were moving to and fro, a dozen cars were going sedately along the street. Mannering dared not shoot.

A police whistle shrilled.

From Piccadilly two constables came rushing. They judged the cause of the trouble quickly, and Mannering saw one of them commandeer a passing car.

The gunman swerved to the pavement, then tried to swing back to the roadway, but the nearside wing crashed into a line of railings, and the gunman was jolted forward, cracking his head against the windscreen. Even then he made a desperate effort to get his gun working, but the policeman who had commandeered the car leapt at him, a truncheon rose and fell, and the gun clattered to the floor of the Morris.

*   *   *

The fierce rush of action from the time Ffoulkes had opened

the door had driven all thought of Clayton from Mannering's mind. Ten minutes passed before he was able to get back to the flat, accompanied by Tanker Tring.

The door of the flat was still open, but he could see neither Ffoulkes nor Bristow.

It was then that he remembered Clayton.

His heart turned over as the possibility of discovery flooded his mind. If Bristow had carried Ffoulkes into the bedroom Clayton would have been found, and all hope of avoiding an open quarrel with the police would be gone.

In a cold sweat, he pushed roughly past Tring. Ffoulkes, with Bristow and a doctor beside him, was stretched out on the sofa.

'I wasn't sure whether he ought to be moved,' Bristow was muttering. 'I thought you'd better see him first. Shall I ring for an ambulance?'

'A moment,' said the doctor. 'Some water, hot if possible, and towels. We'll see what the damage is.'

'Bowl and hot water in the bathroom, Tring,' said Mannering, his nerves steadier. 'By the way, they got the man, Bill.'

'So they got him, did they?' Bristow snapped, his eyes glittering. 'Think it was meant for you?'

'If you must talk,' said the doctor, a grey-haired man now on his knees beside Ffoulkes, 'go somewhere else, but get me that water first. You'll have to ring for an ambulance, I think.'

Bristow forgot his question, and reached for the telephone. Tring could be seen, coming heavily laden from the bathroom, and Mannering chose that opportunity for going into the bedroom. Another dose of chloroform would do Clayton no harm, and the youth must be kept quiet until the flat was empty.

Mannering slipped through, closing the door behind him, then stood staring at the bed. For it was empty.

Chapter 13
The Baron at Work

The long years spent in meeting emergency quickly and without panic, helped Mannering then.

He picked up the dressing-gown cord, straightened the coverlet of the bed, flung wider the already open window to clear the smell of chloroform.

Clayton had recovered, of course, and taken the easiest way out.

But such behaviour was not in character; Mannering would have expected the youngster to come blundering into the living-room, roaring for his assailant's blood. Why had he not done so?

Mannering pushed thought of him aside, and slipped back to the others.

Bristow had finished telephoning, and the doctor was bathing Ffoulkes's temple. Tring was standing by, melancholy and worried.

'Well?' enquired Bristow anxiously, as the doctor deftly wound a bandage into place.

'I can't do any more, Inspector, but I think he'll be all right. There'll have to be an operation, but it should be quite a minor one. I'll look after him myself – you sent to the London Clinic, of course?'

'Yes.' Bristow's tension eased. 'Well, it might have been worse, I suppose. Now I'll be off to Cannon Row. I won't want you just now, Mannering, but I'd like you to be here until you hear from me.'

'In the circumstances,' said Mannering, 'I won't argue about that.'

Bristow left just before the ambulance men arrived. Tring went with him, and the doctor travelled with Ffoulkes. The fingerprint men and photographers were still busy downstairs, and it was an hour before the police left. Mannering brewed himself some tea, put the tray on a table at his side, and sat back to work order out of chaos.

Several things explained themselves.

Ffoulkes, of course, had been shot in mistake for him. It was, knowing Grunfeld, the natural corollary to the telephone conversation.

But the major question remained: who had the other four stars?

It was reasonable – a fact virtually admitted by Grunfeld – to assume that he had stolen the stars for Vincenne; but Grunfeld also admitted *killing* Vincenne.

While someone else had stolen the stars from Vincenne, someone who had put paste gems in their place.

The more recent mysteries also irked Mannering. He reviewed them in order.

1. Where was Annette?
2. Why had Clayton slipped out by the window?
3. How had Legrand known that Duval and Garston would meet to exchange the money for the star?

Grunfeld was looking for the stars, and yet it seemed that he had learned Garston – or Duval – had one for sale, had actually obtained the money for it through Leverson. The most likely assumption was that Duval's connection with the stars was known to Grunfeld, and that Legrand had followed the Frenchman.

'No,' Mannering ejaculated. 'That can't be. Duval wasn't followed. Therefore, Legrand was watching Garston.'

Garston's part loomed more largely as he pondered it.

It was reasonable to assume that he had handled the star Duval had sold, and it was at least likely that he knew where the other four were.

'More than likely,' said Mannering aloud. 'It's as nearly certain as can be, and I'll drop in on him tonight, wiring or no wiring, Bristow or no Bristow.'

The decision cheered him, and he felt easier in his mind. The problem of Annette and Clayton seemed less important; apparently the youngster was in love, and his secondary part in the robbery, his virtual acquiescence in the theft, naturally made him afraid of the police – and explained his hurried getaway from the flat. Moreover, the girl could easily be forgiven for her outburst of the previous night. Odd how that had affected him, Mannering thought.

He moved restlessly. Until he heard from Lynch or Bristow, he could not decently leave the flat, and he looked impatiently at his watch from time to time.

77

It was nearly six when the front door bell rang.

He stood up slowly, wondered whether Legrand would dare to try the same thing twice; and his left hand was closed about his automatic as he approached the door and started to open it.

The agitated breathing of a woman outside reminded him sharply of Annette.

He was prepared to see her as he opened the door wider but he was wrong. It was not Annette Vincenne, but Janet – Leverson's maid – who stood there, her face strained and pale, her breast heaving.

'Janet – what – '

She almost stumbled into the room, and he had to grasp her shoulder to steady her. He had felt uneasy about the old fence, and now that uneasiness crystallised. Again he felt the menace of Grunfeld and Legrand, and a cold, blind anger in his mind towards them.

'Mr Mannering, you've got to find him! I – '

'Drink this,' said Mannering, and he pushed a whisky-and-soda into her shaking hand. 'The quicker I know what's happened the sooner I can help.'

She touched her lips with the whisky, and went on: 'Two – two men called and forced their way in. I couldn't do a thing ... They took him . . . I heard him say he didn't know where the stars were, but they wouldn't listen – ' She stopped, tried to be more coherent. 'I daren't go to the police. I – I knew you'd help.'

'I will,' said Mannering, and he hid from her the hopelessness that filled him. 'I'll get busy right away. You hurry back to the house, and if Mr Leverson should turn up telephone me at once.'

He had warned Flick, and the fence himself had been emphatic enough about Legrand's character and what could be expected of him. It was more evidence of the ruthless thoroughness of the Grunfeld organisation.

The telephone rang sharply. It was Bristow.

'The A.C.'ll pull through,' he said with relief and satisfaction. 'But' – his tone changed to one of disappointment – 'the gunman knows nothing. Merely a tool.'

'What's his story?'

'Oh, common enough. A Paris thug smuggled over here, who takes orders by telephone. But we've several lines we're going to try, and we won't need you just yet.'

'Permission to go out granted?' smiled Mannering.

'By day, and as Mannering,' said Bristow darkly.

'Thank you, Bill,' said Mannering meekly.

But he knew quite well that visiting Mr Matthew Garston that night would – if the police discovered it – bring the whole force of the Yard against him. They distrusted his motives in the affair of the stars, and were alert for any intimation that he was playing some deep game of his own under cover of it.

Yet if ever there was a time when the Baron's work was justified, it was now.

Vincenne – Annette – Ffoulkes – and now Leverson.

There was only one way of helping Leverson, and it led through Garston. He could have told the police what he knew of the man, but there was nothing they could have acted on, for he could not tell the truth of the Garston contact without incriminating Leverson as a fence.

It had to be done on his own.

He left the flat, and went to Fuller Mansions, taking with him all he might need for the night's escapade.

Leaving the luggage at the flat he went on to the house off the Lower Richmond Road. In the gathering dusk it seemed lonely and well away from its neighbours, but there was no chance at all of making a preliminary inspection. He had to work blind and he had to work fast, for he did not think Leverson would survive long, if left to the mercy of Grunfeld and Legrand.

* * *

At one o'clock the traffic was negligible. Mannering drove a small Morris saloon, parking it outside the garage where he had hired the taxi, and continued on foot to the cul-de-sac.

No lights showed from any of the houses.

He felt a rising excitement as he moved towards Leeminx. The Baron was in action, and although he had taken every precaution open to him, he knew that the risks of breaking-in had never been greater.

He had discarded the blue scarf for the night, wearing a black one in its place, and although he carried a gas-pistol in his pocket he would use it only in an emergency. The other tools he carried in a waistband kit might have belonged to any expert cracksman, and could not be identified as the Baron's if he should be forced to leave them behind.

He reached the gateway, all thought – but that of the business in hand – suspended. The gate opened without a sound, and he left it open before walking along the grass verge of the short carriageway towards the house itself.

He examined the front windows. They were neither curtained nor fitted with drawn blinds, and to his expert eye it seemed that the house was without particular precautions against burglary. Yet he distrusted appearances, and in any case preferred to work from the rear of the house.

A side window offered more promise.

With gloved hands the Baron took from his tool-kit a thin-bladed screwdriver, inserting it near the catch. Holding the flat steel handle between his thumb and forefinger, he pushed gently.

And then he felt a sharp, biting pain run through his fingers and up his arm!

He gasped aloud with the sudden pain and snatched his hand from the steel. For fully half-a-minute he was conscious of nothing but the agony of that contact, as he stared at the innocent-seeming window.

Garston's house *was* wired; a considerable voltage of electricity must be running through the steel catch.

This increased the difficulties, yet it also increased the need for getting inside, for it proved that Garston must have a very powerful reason indeed for taking such precautions.

The Baron took stock of the situation. His right hand and arm were numb, and he wondered how long it would be before they returned to normal. He heard no sound from the house nor the streets about it, and he wondered why Garston did not have a system which not only kept intruders out but raised an alarm.

From the start this affair had revealed a thoroughness appalling in its efficiency, and he did not believe that the man who had installed the electric live-wire would stop halfway. The inference, and it was an unpleasant one, was that Garston, or some member of the household, *had* been roused and was waiting in readiness.

In normal circumstances the Baron would have admitted the task to be too dangerous for completing that night, and waited. But as he thought passed through his mind he seemed to see Leverson, quiet and ageing, contented at Wine Street in his virtual retirement. If Grunfeld could treat Minx with such callous brutality, what would he do with Leverson?

Stepping back from the house, Mannering looked upwards, seeing, against the starred sky, two gabled arches.

The easiest way in might be from the roof.

Very carefully Mannering made his way to a small tool-shed at the side of the house. A padlock secured the door, and this he forced with little trouble. The *click!* as the lock went back seemed loud, and he paused, waiting and tense for any sound of approach.

None came.

He pulled the door open and stepped inside, closing it behind him. The thin line of light from his pencil-torch fell on the rungs of a ladder. He examined it more closely. It was in two pieces, would be some twenty-four feet high when extended. It was unwieldly to carry, but he lugged it back to the house, fitted it, and reared it nearest to the lowest point of the roof.

There was no sound but the rustle of the wind.

For the first time he took the black scarf from his pocket and tied it about his neck, ready, in a moment of emergency, to be drawn over his face.

He climbed up quickly.

Keeping his balance with his left hand against the ladder, his feet firmly planted on a rung near the top, he unwound a thin, strong rope from his waist. It was knotted at one-foot intervals, and with it he would be able to get down from any part of the roof most convenient on his return.

For the moment he fitted a small steel hook to one end of it, and then gently tossed the hook towards the gables above him.

Once he overthrew, and the steel hit against tiles.

The next throw fell short, and the hook dragged against the brickwork.

The sound seemed to echo and ring in the Baron's ears, and he waited rigidly, lips set tightly. His heart was pounding as he stood there, but the seconds passed and no other sound reached him. He measured the distance to the gable again, and tossed the hook. This time it fell squarely on to the wood. He tugged at it with as much force as he could muster, but it did not budge.

The most dangerous moment was now at hand.

He supported himself with the rope, leaving both hands off the ladder, and stretched upwards as far as possible while keeping the rope taut. Then he tensed his arms and drew himself upwards, his feet moving clear of the rungs.

The rope itself would hold him.

But was the hook firm enough in the gables, and would the wood hold?

Inch by inch –

Hand over fist he went, closer to the roof with every movement, swaying a little to and fro, scraping his shoes and knees against the brickwork. The strain on his arm-muscles was increasing and he felt the weakness in his right wrist; it was growing numb again. Tight-lipped he stretched upwards to get purchase with his left hand on the gable, but it did not quite reach.

He took a chance.

He released his left hand, felt his right slipping, and hung there with only his left arm to support him, facing failure, knowing it was useless to try to rely on his right.

There was only one chance left.

Carefully he wound the rope about his waist, tying the end that had dangled almost to the concrete, and then he hung from it, pushing his feet against the wall and not using his hands. Almost at right-angles to the wall he used his left hand to pull himself up a few inches, and then moved his feet nearer to the roof.

His foot slipped and he lost ground.

Patiently he started again.

The absence of sound and the fact that no one could see him gave him confidence. It was a challenge to the Baron, and something more: he must not give up trying, Leverson's life was at stake.

At last he gripped the gables with his left hand, put one knee on the edge of the roof and pulled himself up and over. For a moment he lay on the sloping tiles, breathing hard; he rested for three minutes, and then knelt up and looked about him. The faint light from the stars showed him that there was room to walk without danger, he had no need to worry about that. He pulled the hook out of the gabled wood, wound the rope about his waist again, and then started forward.

He wanted to see a roof-light, or the door of a fire-escape; both were possibilities, but he could not be sure of finding either. He went cautiously, sometimes lying at full length against the tiles, at other times walking upright or crouching when the higher points of the roof threatened to reveal him to anyone who might glance up.

Then he saw a small, square patch of frosted glass, fitted into a framework nearly two feet square.

He sat back on his haunches, his eyes gleaming.

The roof-light would be protected, there was no doubt of that, but Mannering believed there was a way of avoiding the likeliest obstacle — the electric wiring. Now that he was able to work on the actual entry he moved swiftly but deliberately. From his tool-kit he took a diamond cutter, a short length of rubber hose, and a small suction cup. He damped the cup with a small sponge and stuck it against the glass, fastened the hose on to it by a screw-connection, and tied one end of the hose about his wrist. That finished, he cut quickly at the glass.

The diamond squealed, but there was little danger of being heard, and he did not pause.

As he made the final cut he felt the glass sag against his fingers, but he prevented it from falling and then slowly lifted the glass square out.

Gently he laid it on a flat stretch of roof.

That finished, he used his pencil-torch again. It shone on a dusty floor, a few packing cases and several trunks.

All he had to make sure of was that he did not touch the wiring.

He climbed through the roof-light, gripping the rope ladder which was coiled round his left wrist, and lowered himself gently. It seemed a long time before his feet touched the bare boards, but at last he was inside and apparently undetected.

Groping forward he located the door, and very softly turned the handle. It was locked.

The Baron frowned as he examined it in the light of his torch.

It was a modern Landon lock, both expensive and effective, one more likely to be found on a safe or study door than that of a loft-room.

Strange.

The Baron pushed the matter to the back of his mind, for the slow start to the exploit made speed more essential, and he was still not absolutely certain that no alarm had been raised. He slipped his gas-pistol into his right-side pocket, and a loaded Webley ·32 in his left, knowing that to carry a loaded gun was to invite trouble, and if the worst happened and he were caught it would double the gravity of his crime.

He set the thought aside, and worked on the lock. Pulling his scarf over his face, he opened the door. A dim light greeted him. He stepped softly towards it, his rubber-soled shoes making no sound.

The light, he found, was at the head of a short flight of stairs. These he descended, finding himself faced with yet another door.

And another Landon lock.

The second Landon brought the puzzle of the first one back to him; he could no longer ignore the implication. There was something of value at the top of the house – something Garston did not propose to leave unguarded.

Time, however, was of utmost importance, and Mannering pressed on.

Opening the second door at last, he peered through. He saw nothing but a small, square room that was unfurnished, and went inside.

Suddenly Garston's voice, metallic and menacing, came to him.

'*I knew there was someone around. Bring him in.*'

A warning had been raised, then, by his contact with the

wire; they knew he was there.

Mannering waited, his eyes narrowed behind his mask, his heart thumping. Footsteps echoed from the far side of the open door, and then he heard Garston again:

'*Hurry, damn you!*'

No other voice answered, and Garston's was on a very low key. An idea passed through Mannering's mind, and another in quick succession. The second seemed incredible, but the first was reasonable enough; it sounded as if Garston was speaking into a telephone.

He opened the door six inches wider, and saw that it was so. Garston sat not a yard from him, with a hand-microphone.

The second idea had support, yet it was hard to believe. Mannering looked over his shoulder, made sure that he was not being followed, that his presence was unsuspected.

Someone besides the Baron?

There could be no other explanation. Another intruder had visited Leeminx, the alarm he, Mannering, had raised had warned Garston, and the other man had suffered.

Footsteps, much nearer.

A tap sounded on the door in front of Garston.

'All right, come in.'

Two men entered, dragging another man.

'Put him there,' said Garston.

He motioned to a couch on one side of the room, and then gave orders for the prisoner's hands and feet to be tied. Mannering waited on tenterhooks, trying to see the prisoner's face, wondering if the odd chance had turned up and the prisoner was Leverson.

Then Garston stood up, enabling Mannering to see the face of the unconscious prisoner: and if by nothing else he would have recognised the man by the livid scar that ran from his lips to his left ear.

It was Duval!

Chapter 15
Quick Getaway

The Frenchman's head lolled back, and at his temple was an ugly bruise.

Why was Duval here?

Questions, always questions; and there was no chance, as yet, of finding answers for them. Mannering kept his eyes glued to the narrow opening of the door, and his hand about his gas-pistol. He watched Garston bend over the prisoner, and heard him say:

'All right, clear out and wait outside. I know this joker, we may have to put him away.'

Garston stood for a moment above Duval, and then slapped his hand across the other's face.

'Wake up, you runt!'

Duval stirred and grunted. Garston took a carafe of water from the desk at which he had been sitting, and dashed it into the Frenchman's face. Duval's eyes opened, and he started up at Garston.

Mannering saw cold hatred in his gaze.

Garston said abruptly: 'How'd you find this place?'

Duval's tongue ran along his lips, but not in fear.

'I – read the card.' His English was good, the words well pronounced.

'You did, did you?'

'I came,' Duval said, 'to get what is mine, Gar-ston. In that envelope was nothing – '

Garston laughed, and suddenly Mannering understood the reason for Duval's visit. The man had exchanged an envelope for Leverson's eight thousand pounds, an envelope that should have contained Duval's share of the deal. Instead it had been empty.

Duval, sharp-witted enough to read the address while the policeman had copied it from the card, had come on an errand of vengeance; and Mannering's sympathies were all with him.

'What if it *was* blank paper?' sneered Garston. 'You'd have been a lot better off with that than you're going to be now!'

Contempt lay in Duval's eyes, but no fear. Mannering felt a liking and an admiration for the man who must believe that his position was hopeless, and yet showed no sign of cringing.

Garston said brutally: 'There's only one thing might help you, and that is if you can tell me where the stars are.'

Mannering heard the words with a shock of surprise.

Garston did not know where the other stars were!

There was a long drawn-out silence, enabling Mannering to adjust his mind to that discovery.

Garston and Grunfeld worked separately –

Confirmation came of that almost immediately.

'It was Legrand who took the money. He might know – ' Duval spoke wearily, as if he cared nothing what happened.

'Oh, I know all about Legrand and that swine Grunfeld, don't you worry.'

'*I* do not worry.'

'Just as well you don't,' said Garston, and Mannering could imagine the ugly grin on his lips. 'You're going for a long ride – '

He turned sharply towards the far door.

And then the Baron moved.

He pushed open the door.

Duval saw him, and his eyes widened. Before Garston could make a sound the Baron reached him; his left hand went to the other's throat, dragging him off balance, choking the words back. Slowly Mannering forced him backwards, increasing the pressure.

He had been reluctant to use his gas-pistol, but the only chance of a getaway for himself and Duval was to keep Garston silent for some minutes. The concentrated ether-gas was the only weapon at hand; the risk had to be taken.

As Garston drew in a strangled breath, Mannering pressed the bulb of the gas-pistol. A charge of ether-gas, highly concentrated, was drawn into Garston's lungs. For a moment he lunged unavailingly – and then he collapsed, fading into unconsciousness.

The Baron glanced at Duval, and lifted a hand for silence.

From his waistband he took a length of fine cord and fastened Garston securely, then pushed the man into the chair at the desk and turned to Duval; his voice was a whisper:

'Say nothing, just follow me.'

Duval nodded as the Baron first cut through the cords that bound him, then lifted Garston bodily, and carried him into

87

the empty room.

Duval followed.

'A chair,' Mannering whispered.

Duval brought one, Garston was pushed into it and then Mannering closed the door. He spoke softly.

'Wait there, and let me know if you hear a sound – we may want good time to get away.'

'I – understand,' Duval said.

He had taken the development with a quiet coolness that Mannering admired as he had done the earlier stoical resignation, and he took his stand by the door, alert and ready for emergency.

Garston stirred and his eyes flickered open.

The Baron, still wearing his black scarf, stood over him.

And then Garston jolted him severely.

'You – you're the – the Baron,' he muttered. 'That gas – God, I – '

Few who knew of the Baron were unaware of the gas-pistol, and Mannering knew that the odds were building up against him. But his task for the moment was to learn what he could.

'Don't try to get away,' he said sharply, 'it won't help you. You know Grunfeld, don't you?'

'Yes.' Garston leaned forward, straining against his bonds.

'When did you last hear from him?'

'This – this morning. I – '

'Where was he?'

'At – at Lambeth.'

'How do I get to it?'

Terror returned to Garston's eyes, as if he realised that unless he gave an answer he would get no mercy.

'I – I don't know, I swear I don't, I've been there twice but they always make me wear dark glasses, I don't know – '

'He's got other places, hasn't he?' snapped the Baron.

'He – yes, his house, he – '

'Where?'

'In – in Battersea. Eighteen – Lorler Drive. He – '

'What's his name there?'

'Greenfield, Lew Greenfield!'

Mannering said: 'Just what is your business with Grunfeld?' and his voice grew softer and yet more menacing. Every tinge of colour drained from Garston's face.

'I – I daren't – '

'*Boss. Boss!*'

The words came clearly even through the two closed doors, so sharply and suddenly that Mannering jumped round and Duval tightened his grip on the door handle.

Together they went into the study, and Mannering spoke in a good imitation of Garston's metallic voice.

'What's that row about?'

'Boss, there's a ladder outside! Someone else –'

Mannering swore, as Garston would have done.

His mind was alert to handle this new threat, the fact that his method of entry had been discovered. He had feared that development from the first. The youth had told him Garston always had two menservants, but that was no guarantee that others were not on the premises. He had to make sure now.

'Get round to the ladder, fast, you fools!'

'That's okay, Tig and Benny are there. The guy must be on the roof, we can get him through your room –'

'All right,' grated Mannering, and he stepped towards the door, motioning Duval towards the other side of it.

Duval jumped to the next move without hesitation. Mannering would open it and let the men rush in – two against two would be easy enough to handle. But as he touched the door knob a thought flashed through his mind. He doubled back to Garston, unceremoniously running through his pockets for wallet, keys and papers, then back to the door, this time the automatic in his hand.

Two men on the threshold took a step forward – and then they saw the gun and Mannering, and reared backwards, stupefaction on their faces.

'Gawd!'

The Baron moved back a pace, lifting his left hand towards Duval; but the signal was not necessary, for Duval moved fast.

He struck savagely, a blow both scientific and certain; the rough-neck crumpled up, and while he was falling the second man was struck. Mannering stepped over their inert bodies; and as he did so, a voice travelled upwards from the floor below, deep and gruff, so obviously that of a policeman that Mannering felt a cold shiver of apprehension.

'What's 'appening here?'

'A moment, constable!' Mannering raised his voice and gripped Duval's arm with his left hand.

'Hit him,' Mannering whispered, 'but not too hard. Clear?'

Duval nodded.

Mannering hurried towards the stairs, knowing that the last chance of looking through Garston's house had gone for that night.

A thickset, heavily moustached constable was peering stolidly upwards.

'I heard a row, and the door was open –'

'Yes, visitors, I'm afraid.' Mannering spoke as Mr Moore would have done, his voice was not recognisable as Mannering's. 'I – behind you, constable!'

The policeman turned – and Duval tipped his helmet forward on his head. The blow hit the nape of the bared neck, not heavily, but enough to ensure unconsciousness. Mannering stopped the man from falling, and lowered him quickly.

'Nicely done, Duval. I –'

And then footsteps sounded above them, and they heard Garston's voice. Mingling with this was the sound of the two men who had been sent to investigate the ladder. There was not a moment to spare.

Mannering and Duval raced to the hall and through the open doorway. The silent street greeted them, but the footsteps of their pursuers made noise enough.

'Turn left,' Mannering called.

Duval obeyed, the Baron hot on his heels. They reached the main road, no more than fifty yards behind them.

Mannering leapt into the driving-seat of the Morris, setting the car into motion as the three men turned into the Lower Richmond Road.

The car swung into the roadway. Something heavy crashed against the wing, but did no damage, and the engine roared as Mannering trod on the accelerator. The last glimpse he had of the three men was as they stood helplessly, glaring towards the disappearing car.

He felt light-hearted with the relief from tension. And then, like a douche of cold water, he remembered that Garston had recognised him as the Baron.

There was a fairly good chance that Garston, almost certainly wary of the police, would make light of the raid. Nevertheless Mannering knew that the threat of impending disaster hovered about him. There was nothing he could do to stop it if it came, no way in which it could be avoided.

Duval spoke as they reached Chelsea Town Hall.

'Where do you take me, *M'sieu?*'

'Somewhere to talk,' said Mannering, sombrely.

'As you say,' Duval said quietly. 'You are, in truth the Baron?'

Mannering's lips tightened. Of what use was it to deny it now?

'So unlike my imaginings of him,' Duval went on. 'And – so much like a man I saw this morning, yes? But I forget that if you wish it; I owe you much.'

'I'm hoping,' said Mannering quietly, 'that you're going to pay me back, Duval.'

They reached the flat in silence.

Duval glanced about the luxuriously furnished room and lifted his hands expressively. There was a glint of humour in his eyes as he regarded Mannering.

'The world is good for the Baron,' he said. 'I gave you the congratulations, *M'sieu*. And now, what is it that you would talk about?'

'Garston, primarily,' said Mannering, 'and the star. But before we go into that I'll look through Garston's papers. He may have had something worthwhile in his pockets.'

Duval nodded, and Mannering took out Garston's wallet and the loose papers. The latter proved unimportant; two private letters and a garage bill. The wallet held an Automobile Association membership card, three five-pound bank notes and a thin leather case about the size of a post-card.

Mannering unfolded the case.

The face of Minx, startlingly lifelike, looked up at him.

Chapter 16
Ebb and Flow

The Baron put the photograph down slowly, trying to realise what it might mean.

'You – know the mam'selle?'

Mannering had forgotten Duval's presence, and jumped at the slow, quiet voice.

'I've seen her,' he said, 'but there's something else of importance, Duval. I – can you make coffee?'

'Of course.'

Mannering waved his hand in the direction of the kitchen.

'You'll find everything there. I have to make a telephone call. Leave the door open if you prefer it.'

With a certain delicacy, Duval closed the door of the kitchenette.

Mannering picked up the London directory, and found the number of Mr Greenfield of 18 Lorler Drive, Battersea.

The telephone burred in his ear for two minutes without an answer. Mannering scowled, reminded himself that Grunfeld was probably at Lambeth, and then dialled the number again.

He would have preferred to make a visit as the Baron, but there was no time that night, and he was sure that Grunfeld's precautions against burglary would be even more thorough than Garston's. Breaking in at Battersea woud need time and preparation; and he had to work immediately if he were to save Leverson.

Three minutes passed, and then a voice came over the wire, alert and familiar. *Legrand's !*

'Who is that?'

'My name doesn't matter,' said Mannering, and he used the voice of Mr Moore. 'I wish to talk with Mr Greenfield.'

'It is impossible, he is not to be disturbed.'

'It concerns Mannering,' said Mannering sharply.

There was a heavy silence, then: 'I will advise him, please hold on.'

Mannering waited, and at last Grunfeld's voice came

gratingly over the wire.

'Hallo.'

'Well, well,' said Mannering, and his voice was his own. 'Not *quite* so clever as you thought you were, eh? How is Annette?'

'You –'

'Swear by all means, if it helps you,' Mannering said indulgently, 'but understand this.' His voice sharpened. 'Both Annette and Leverson are to be freed within an hour, or – the police come to Battersea.'

'How can I, if I don't know where the little fool is? Blast her!'

'No? You arranged for her to move from Streatham.'

'Supposing I did? The devil alone knows where she is now. I don't.'

In the sudden desperation in the other's voice, Mannering heard the truth. It suggested that Grunfeld not only feared a police call at Battersea, but that he dared not risk one that night.

Mannering said: 'Well, concentrate on Leverson. You're to let him go.'

Grunfeld sneered: 'What's John Mannering got to do with a jewel-fence? My God, I –'

Mannering said coldly: 'Leverson and I are old friends. He's been out of the game for years, he would not have handled the star but for my interest. You really can't afford to make any *further* mistakes, Grunfeld. Have Leverson put in a taxi at Westminster Bridge within the hour. If he hasn't telephoned me half-an-hour after that, I'll be calling the Yard.'

'And how do I know you won't call them anyway?'

'You just have to hope,' said Mannering.

He rang off quickly, and stared ahead of him. Had it been a mistake to admit his friendship with the fence? He believed not, and that the only additional risk at the moment was from the police interrogation of Garston at Leeminx.

It was impossible, of course, to be sure that Leverson would be freed, but he believed the fence would have no further trouble. At least there was nothing more he could do that morning, and he felt tired, jaded.

Garston – Grunfeld – Minx – Annette.

Duval.

At least he would soon know what Duval could tell him, for

the Frenchman with the scar came from the kitchen, a tray in his right hand.

'Once, *M'sieu*, I was to be a *maitre d'hotel*. It gives pleasure to serve the Baron – *le Maitre* of the Night. White, *M'sieu*, or black?'

* * *

Duval, it seemed, had spent five years in London, at a Piccadilly Hotel, before returning to France and becoming involved, through a woman, in a fracas that had ruined his looks and his prospects as a hotelier. He discussed that briefly and dispassionately.

Mannering found it easy to believe his story. The *Sûreté* wanting him on suspicion of a shop robbery; Duval had been compelled to leave Paris in a hurry. In need of money quickly he had been put in touch with Garston.

Garston had handed over the star and told him to negotiate with Leverson.

'I was,' Duval said, 'to receive one hundred pounds, *M'sieu*. Garston tricked me, gave me waste paper. I had read his address, and I was determined to make him pay. The rest you know.'

'You must have arrived five minutes after I did,' said Mannering, as Duval poured out coffee. 'Well – that seems to be that. Do you know anything of Legrand?'

'Only that he is a bad man, *M'sieu*, much wanted in France.'

'Grunfeld?'

'I know him not.'

'Well, the only hope is the man who put you in touch with Garston. Can you find him again?'

'I can try, *M'sieu*.'

'Do, tomorrow. There's no reason why you should not sleep here tonight, but I'm leaving. Bring a written message to this address – Flat 29, Fuller Mansions – if you can get the man or news about him, and – ' He took his wallet out and selected a twenty-pound note. 'This can be part of the hundred, the other's to come.'

'*M'sieu* has no need to do that,' said Duval quickly. 'There is money in Garston's wallet, it can serve until I find other work. Please, *M'sieu*.'

'My dear Duval,' said Mannering gently, 'Legrand did not get away with Garston's eight thousand. I was there, and it changed hands twice.'

The keen eyes narrowed and then gleamed with laughter. Duval took the notes, folded them, and bowed.

'Truly *le Maitre*,' he said. 'It would be the pleasure to work with you. You will, I hope, remember that.'

And the Baron knew that it was an offer of help – help he might need badly before the affair was over.

* * *

Leverson's voice sounded very tired.

'I can't thank you enough, John, I thought – oh, well, it doesn't matter. Is there anything I can tell you?'

From Brook Street, Mannering said: 'Just what happened?'

'I was taken to Lambeth – I assume it was the place you'd seen – and questioned. Grunfeld wanted the other stars, of course. It – it wasn't pleasant. How did you manage it?'

'Thanks chiefly to Duval,' said Mannering, at once relieved to know the fence was free and filled with a cold anger at the inference in Leverson's words.

'John – can't you drop the whole thing? These people aren't normal.'

'No,' said Mannering, slowly. 'I can't back out now. It's gone too far. Did you hear anything of the girl Annette?'

'Enough to know that they caught her and lost her – they thought she was unconscious but she slipped out of the car, and managed to get free.'

'Well – I'm – damned!' exclaimed Mannering. 'All right, Flick, I won't keep you any longer. Goodnight, old man.'

It was nearly five o'clock when Mannering rang off, and he was asleep within ten minutes.

* * *

At it proved, Mannering was right in his assumption that Garston would play down the break-in to the police. For a burglary concerning the Baron would earn far more attention than Matthew Garston wanted.

The Inspector went off finally, to make his report, promising to send round another man in the morning. At five o'clock Garston went to his study, nervously apprehensive of any repercussion that might – that *would* – follow the giving away of Grunfeld's address.

* * *

Some forty miles from London, at the time Mannering was

preparing for his visit to Garston's house, Annette Vincenne stared mutinously at young Clayton.

'I cannot see why I should be so frightened of the police, always the police! They know nothing!'

'They might learn a lot. If you don't show up they'll have every damned policeman in the country looking for you. Mannering said – '

'Mannering, Mannering! But for him this would not have happened, he can talk, yes, it seems he has talked to you!'

Clayton's voice grew quieter, gentler.

'Darling, I'm awfully sorry about the way things have gone, but there's nothing that can be helped, you know, and I'm doing everything I can.'

'Pah! The police, even Mannering, do more than you. Tell me, what have *you* done except to follow me?'

'It's a good job I did. If I hadn't been following you this morning where'd you have been when you jumped out of that car? Hang it, Annette, if you don't go to the police those fellows might come again.'

She looked suddenly very forlorn and very lonely.

'Yes. The man with the black eyes – he was enough to frighten anyone, Richard. He – I dare not move from here! I have found this place, and I stay until – until the men who killed my father are found. Not until then will I be safe!'

'You'd be a lot safer with the police looking after you than stuck in a country pub,' said Clayton heatedly.

'I stay here!' Annette snapped, and then she left her chair and stretched her arms out to Clayton. 'Richard, please don't get angry, I'm frightened, *so* frightened – '

*　　*　　*

Towards noon on the day after Leverson had been released, Grunfeld entered the small bedroom on the lower floor of the Lambeth apartment.

Minx lifted her head.

Mannering would have been aghast had he seen her. In less than two days she had changed from a vivacious and beautiful girl to a haggard and hollow-eyed wreck.

Lack-lustre, spiritless, she said: 'One little shot, Lew, only one – '

'Get some clothes on,' Grunfeld said, 'and come upstairs. You can have as much as you like if you do what I tell you – '

'Lew! Lew, I'll do anything, anything, a little shot now

and – just a little one now. Oh, God, I can't stand it without, I can't – '

He shrugged, and took a small piece of white paper from his waistcoat pocket. She snatched at it, opened it quickly, and sniffed hard at the fine white powder there.

In twenty minutes, her eyes sparkling, her beauty back again, she entered the lounge where she had first met Mannering, and where Grunfeld now sat, talking to Legrand.

'Hallo, Minx, there's a present for you.' He pushed towards her a brown-paper packet. 'Now we're all right, aren't we?' He patted her shoulder, breezy and apparently good-natured. 'Now, we've got a problem here we can't work out. Two, as a matter of fact. Mannering's found out where I live at Battersea.'

Minx stared.

'*Mannering* has? How could he?'

'It's done, it's done,' said Grunfeld testily, 'don't let's waste time. Now there's you, Legrand, one or two of the men and Garston who know it. I'm afraid Mannering's got on to Garston and made him talk, but I don't want to deal with Matthew until I'm sure.'

'He – he wouldn't dare to talk.'

'No one would,' said Grunfeld drily, 'but someone has, my dear, don't make any mistake about that.'

'Will Mannering advise the police?' asked Legrand.

'He might,' said Grunfeld sharply. 'On the other hand it might suit him to keep the knowledge up his sleeve for the moment. He works very much on his own, and of course that moment may be long or short. That is why our second problem will be to get him here. Meanwhile, we will deal with Matthew. Minx, I want you to see him this afternoon, and find out if he *did* talk.'

Minx nodded.

'Good girl, I knew you could handle Matthew. Just find out what happened, and get back as soon as you can. And now, my dear, the other thing. I've reason to think Mannering's rather attached to you, Minx – and you did give him a certain amount of encouragement, didn't you?'

Minx said evenly: 'You needn't worry about that again. I wanted him to join up with us, that's why I went to see him.'

'Aren't we wasting a lot of time?' Legrand broke in.

Grunfeld glanced up irritably.

'All right, all right.' He turned back to the girl. 'The thing is, Minx, I want you to go and see Mannering, and tell him that the stars are at Battersea. He'll go after them, and – well, I'm afraid he mustn't get away again. We can't keep making mistakes, that's certain. Think you can do it?'

'Of course.'

'Excellent, excellent,' said Grunfeld. 'Well, off you go to Matthew, and telephone Mannering that you want to see him in the morning. No, this evening – the quicker the better.' He patted her shoulder again, and Minx laughed provocatively.

As the door closed Legrand frowned.

'Are you sure she is reliable, sir?'

'She'll be a sight more reliable than your blasted gunman was,' snapped Grunfeld. 'Anyhow, she won't risk missing her snow again. You can get along and make all the arrangements for Mannering's reception at Battersea. He'll go all right.' Grunfeld laughed, rubbing his hands. 'Mannering very nearly got me worried, Legrand, very nearly.'

Legrand shrugged.

'He acts quickly, that is all. There is more importance in the fact that we have not yet found the stars.'

Grunfeld scowled.

'We will, make no mistake about that. Legrand, you're sure it wasn't Mannering himself who snatched that money from you?'

'It was a middle-aged, rather seedy-looking man, not Mannering's type at all. But you're not forgetting that the money is a side issue?'

'Eight thousand pounds in cash looks a bit more than a side issue to me!'

'Of course, but the important thing is that Garston had one of the stars, or he could not have sold it. He has never told you how he came by it?'

'No. If we have to put him away, we'll ask a few questions first. A pity that damned Vincenne girl slipped our fingers. I think the old man told her practically everything.'

Legrand smiled thinly.

'We can get her again when we want her. Clayton followed her and saw her yesterday evening at a small hotel in Surrey – the "Rose and Crown" at Shere. But we'd better handle Garston and Mannering first, hadn't we?'

Grunfeld chuckled.

'You're right enough, Legrand. You know what to do at Battersea, don't you?'

'A thousand volts ought to be enough,' said Legrand, with a calm viciousness. 'There won't be much of him left after that.'

Chapter 17
Annette Again

'Forgive me, darling,' said Mannering into the telephone. 'It just happened that I couldn't ring through last night, and this morning I've been sleeping late. It's one of the disadvantages of an easy conscience.'

'H'mm. We'll let that go. Is everything all right?'

'I'm making progress. If you were here I would tell you about it.'

'I could be, in three hours,' Lorna said tentatively.

'I'm not risking the chance that they might be your last ones,' said Mannering briskly. 'I'll phone you during the day if I can, but don't get het up if anything stops me coming through. Things all right down there?'

He rang off five minutes later. It was half-past eleven, which meant that he had managed to get nearly six hours sleep. He felt none the worse for his previous night's activity, although he was disappointed that there had been no opportunity of going through Leeminx more thoroughly. There was, of course, the chance of going back. On the other hand, Garston might remove whatever it was he valued so much: one visit from the Baron was enough for most people.

The Baron, thought Mannering, and his good spirits were suddenly gone.

Did Bristow know?

Only a brief mention of the burglary had appeared in print. If the Press had scented the Baron it would have given to it more than a four-line paragraph, and that offered hope.

A telephone call from Bristow reassured him further.

Ffoulkes was progressing well, although he would be *hors de combat* for several weeks.

'Any word of Annette Vincenne?' Mannering asked him.

'No, not a thing, but we had young Clayton in this morning. He hasn't seen her since yesterday before she disappeared.'

'Hasn't, or says he hasn't?'

'We'd no grounds for detaining him,' Bristow said testily, 'although he'll be questioned again, of course. Oh, and we've got the dossier of Legrand from Paris. He's wanted for – '

'Two knife murders, plus,' said Mannering gently.

'How the devil did *you* know?'

'One hears things,' said Mannering airly. 'You don't sound as pleased with life as you should be. Has the Super been a little heavy-handed?'

Bristow grunted.

'He's down with 'flu, the one thing I didn't want just now, and I'm working more or less on my own. All right, Mannering, I'll see you later.'

Mannering replaced the receiver with a certain satisfaction. Lynch and Ffoulkes out of action; of the men at the Yard who knew that Mannering and the Baron were one and the same, only Tring and Bristow remained active.

He thought of Annette and Clayton.

Where was she?

Brrr-brrr!'

He lifted the telephone quickly, and gave his name. A bellow in his ear almost made him drop the instrument.

'Mannering, I've got to see you!'

'So it's you, is it?' Mannering's voice sounded casual enough, but to hear from young Clayton at that particular moment was just what he had wanted.

'Listen! I've found Annette, but she's being so damned silly. Perhaps *you* might be able to persuade her to have some sense. Will you come with me to see her? We can get to Shere in just over an hour.'

Mannering said sharply: 'You're sure she's there?'

'Of course I'm sure. I phoned her only ten minutes ago. I'll meet you at Hyde Park Corner in twenty minutes, is that all right?'

Mannering said slowly: 'I'm not sure. Go there and wait for me, and if I'm not there in half-an-hour, ring me again. But if you're planning to waste my time, Clayton, I'd think twice about it.'

'Goddam, why should I?' snapped Clayton. 'Can't you see I'm half-crazy with worry about Annette? If the police – '

'Don't tell the world about it,' said Mannering shortly 'I'll try to get over.'

He replaced the receiver, then dialled Flick Leverson's number. Janet's voice answered him.

'I'd like two men useful with their fists if necessary, Janet. Can you get hold of them quickly for me?'

'I think so. Where?'

'Tell them to follow the Frazer Nash in which I shall leave Hyde Park Corner, will you. I'll be there in about half-an-hour.'

'I'll phone right away.'

Mannering loaded his automatic, and slipped it in his pocket. He did not seriously think that Clayton would try any tricks, but the parts the youngster and Annette were playing were sufficiently in doubt to warrant every precaution.

At a quarter-to-one he reached Hyde Park Corner.

The Frazer Nash was already there, with an exceedingly impatient Clayton stamping up and down.

'I thought you were never coming, Mannering.'

'Think yourself lucky I did,' said Mannering shortly.

He said nothing more as they drove out of London, his eye noting with satisfaction the Hillman which was discreetly following.

He spoke at last: 'So you want to forget the flat episode, do you?'

Clayton looked uncomfortable.

'I – oh, hell, I don't want to be mixed up if I can help it. I'm only staying in the business for Annette; I'd let my money go hang. When I saw Bristow in your room I lost my head.'

'A dangerous procedure,' said Mannering drily, 'one shouldn't make a habit of it.'

Mickleham – Box Hill – Dorking. Clayton knew the road well and took no wrong turnings. At precisely two o'clock he pulled up outside a small, attractive looking country inn on a by road leading to Guildford.

Mannering had learnt little more from him than the fact – which he already knew – that Annette had been abducted from Streatham; that he, Clayton, had followed the car from the hotel and that when she had got away he had picked her up. They had driven down here, and then Annette had refused to move another inch.

'And what do you want me to do?' Mannering asked.

'Persuade her to tell the police, of course. Damn it she's in danger, Mannering! Someone thinks she has the other stars, or knows where they are – that's as plain as a pikestaff. Or,' he had added bitingly, 'haven't you got that far yet?'

Mannering repressed a retort with difficulty as he followed Clayton through the hall of the inn and up a flight of twisting stairs. On the landing he banged on the first door, entering almost at once.

Annette was standing by her dressing-table, her hair falling over her shoulders; luxurious hair, so black that it seemed blue. She was staring wide-eyed at the door.

'Richard, I – you!'

Mannering closed the door slowly behind him, looked at Annette's suddenly angry face and glittering eyes, and resisted a temptation to laugh. She was so tiny, so childlike, and so intense – and she hated him, there was no question of that.

'You brought him here!' She swung round on Clayton with her right hand clenched. 'Pig! I told you not to! Get out, get out, get out!'

'Easy now,' said Mannering, soothingly. 'We aren't exactly close friends, Annette, but you should try to believe that I'm trying to help.'

'Help! You killed –'

'And let's have no nonsense,' Mannering said firmly. 'Your father came to me to sell stolen jewels. He told me that you knew all about it, and if the police know *that*, they'll want to talk to you. You seem to be in a fix only partly of your own making, and I'll try to get you out of it – but only if you're reasonable. Is that clear enough?'

She looked about to fly at him – and then she broke down, throwing herself across the bed and sobbing bitterly.

Clayton moved towards her.

'Annette, please!'

'Let her be,' said Mannering quietly. He stood waiting and listening, glancing out of the window but seeing no one except the two men who had followed him. There was no trick coming from Clayton, of that he felt sure.

The paroxysm lasted for ten minutes: another five passed before she sat up and looked wet-eyed at Mannering.

'Now you laugh, eh?'

She had spirit, thought Mannering, for the words came with bravery and defiance. He smiled – and Mannering's smile could be exceedingly attractive.

'No, Annette, there's no cause for laughter. Now, if I'm to help you, I want you to tell me everything you can – and then let the police know where you are. There's no need to tell them anything else.'

'It means questions, always questions!'

'You know,' said Mannering, 'I don't believe you're

frightened of the police – but you're certainly frightened of something. What is it?'

'Richard knows! Those men –'

'Yes, but you were frightened before you saw them.'

She bit her lip.

'I – I was frightened for my father – was there not reason for that? And for myself, and Richard, if the police should know what we helped to do! Understand, twenty-four hours before the death of my father, we saw the stars! Yes, saw them! When they were stolen! Do I want to go to prison, to –'

She broke off, breathing hard. It was very convincing; yet somewhere within him Mannering felt a doubt as to whether she was telling the whole truth.

'I see,' he said. 'You knew, then, that your father had a paste set of the stars in his case?'

'No, no, he did not! Only the real ones!'

If that were so, the mystery of the paste gems remained; was there no way of getting at it, no way of finding the answer?

'All right,' he said. 'Did he try to sell the jewels to anyone else?'

Annette stared.

'But of course – two, three people. They refused.'

Mannering said sharply: 'He showed them the real diamonds?'

'What else would he do?'

If that were true, it widened the field immeasurably. It meant that others had known of the theft before Mannering, any one of them could have followed Vincenne, and changed the stars.

'Who were they?' he asked quietly.

Annette shrugged.

'There was Grionde, in Paris, and a man named Didcotte, an American in England –'

Mannering felt the hope dying, for Grionde was as reliable as Leverson, while he knew Didcotte as a considerable collector of precious stones but the last man in the world to plan any kind of crime like this. One chance remained, the third man's name.

Annette hesitated but at last went on.

'And there was a man named Mat – yes, Matthew Garston. But father, he disliked the man, he would not see him again.'

The belief that Garston had received the star by a roundabout route had been so firmly established in Mannering's mind that Annette's words came as a shock, and he stared hard as if doubting what she told him. Annette lifted her hands as high as her head, and exclaimed with fine scorn:

'Why do you look the fool, eh? Must all the men I know be fools, I ask you that!'

Her indignation was so comic that Mannering laughed, and the tension eased.

'It must be the way you look at them, Annette, but that needn't worry us at the moment. Your father went to Garston, did he, with the stars?'

'Yes, at some place near the river.'

'When was this?'

'The day before he sees you.'

'Did Garston ever hold the stars? For an hour or two, I mean, not for a moment.'

'No, no. My father was there, he told me, only ten-fifteen minutes, and then he went to you.'

'Was there anyone else?'

'No – only you.'

Mannering stepped to the window, gazing, unseeing, at a fine orchard. A credible explanation of the adventures of the star Garston had sold was gradually forming in his mind. From what Annette had told him there was one explanation that was so simple that it could be laughable; it would also explain why the other four stars were missing, why Garston did not know where they were.

For the fact that neither Garston nor Grunfeld knew where to find them seemed pretty conclusive. If Duval was as reliable as Mannering believed, he, also, knew nothing. There were two outside suspects in Annette and Clayton, but that was the limit, except –

Minx, of course; Legrand –

It began to look as if there might have been trickery within

Grunfeld's camp. Mannering turned from the window.

'Well now,' he said heartily, hoping to avoid another scene, 'we seem to have gone as far as we can, except deciding what we're going to do with you.'

'Pah!' said Annette. 'I stay here.'

'That's the one thing you don't do. You'd be much wiser to return to London and tell the police why you ran away.'

'Ran away!' She glared round at him. 'I do what I like M'sieu Mannering, and I do not like the police. They will cover my father's name with – what do you say? – ignominy, mine also. No! No!'

Mannering recognised in the girl an obstinacy which he would not be able to shift by simple persuasion. He had little time to waste with her, and yet he could not leave her here.

He thought of Lorna, who wanted to help, and was less than two hours' run away.

He said pleasantly: 'What about a compromise? Would you like to stay with a friend of mine for a day or two?'

'Friend? Where is she?'

'She's staying in the country,' Mannering said. 'I'll go downstairs to telephone and ask her to fetch you. But understand, Annette' – he looked at her, and she returned his look with an odd mixture of pathos and defiance – 'if there's any more fooling, I'll inform the police at once where you are.'

'It will be so nice to rest,' Annette said; and to Mannering the little sigh that followed was the most convincing utterance he had heard from her.

*　　*　　*

To foist upon Lady Fauntley as well as her daughter a girl who was wanted by the police was not a thing Mannering liked to do; but he could see no other way out, for he believed Annette would break down under another police grilling, and Bon would pounce on her. He arranged with Lorna to fetch the girl from the 'Rose and Crown', and relied on Lorna to give a sufficiently reasonable explanation to her mother.

The arrangements made, he rejoined Annette and Clayton. They looked up at him eagerly, expectantly.

'That's fixed,' he said. 'Annette will stay here until Miss Fauntley comes. You and I are returning to town, Clayton.'

*　　*　　*

Garston was a man who had a considerable opinion of himself, and was ready at all times to explain away any damage to his self-esteem. The loss of eight thousand pounds, the failure of his effort to trick Duval and the burglary by the Baron, had been three telling blows; but his out-manoeuvring of the police, who sent a sergeant for a cursory inspection the morning after the burglary, enabled him to regain some of his complacency.

When an M.G. pulled up outside Leeminx, towards four o'clock that afternoon, Garston was at ease in the drawing-room, drinking tea. He heard the squeal of brakes, glanced out, and saw Minx. He hurried to meet her.

'Matthew, it's good to see you!'

'I'll say it's good!' exclaimed Garston, gripping her hands and drawing her to him. 'Let's have a good look at you. Sam, bring another pot of tea and some scones.' Garston hitched his chair nearer to Minx. 'How are things at Lambeth?'

She laughed lightly.

'All right, Matt.'

'No trouble?'

'None,' said Minx dispassionately. 'He doesn't know that I'm any more than a casual friend of yours. What's worrying you?'

'Me worried?' Garston guffawed. 'Don't run away with that idea, Minx. I don't let anything get me down. Had a spot of bother last night, though.'

'Bother? Matt, nothing dangerous – ?'

'Someone got an idea I had the other stars, I suppose. Anyway, the *Baron* looked in.'

Minx stared in slowly dawning comprehension. It was clear enough to her that the Baron had forced him to talk of the house in Battersea.

She spoke sharply.

'What did you tell him, Matthew? What did he want?'

'Oh, forget – '

'I can't! That man's dangerous, if anything should happen to you I don't know what I would do!'

Lying to Garston, she knew, was the easiest of tasks; his vanity enabled him to take anything that savoured of a compliment at its face value. Minx, of course, had learned that he had bought a star and was selling to Leverson through Duval; all Legrand had needed to do was to follow Garston, even though the snatch had not worked to plan.

In three minutes Minx knew the truth, knew that the Baron

107

had learned of Grunfeld's Battersea address.

The Baron –

But it was *Mannering* who had telephoned 'Greenfield' little more than an hour after the Baron had left Putney!

* * *

'The Baron, eh?' said Grunfeld thoughtfully. 'It's damned funny. Don't you think so, Legrand?'

'From the first I have felt there was something mysterious about Mannering,' said Legrand. 'Something I could not understand. This might be it.'

'But he – he's friendly with the police, he's in the best Society,' protested Minx. 'It isn't possible!'

'Oh, it's possible all right,' said Grunfeld. 'Of course, Mannering and the Baron might just know each other. Mannering's a collector and maybe not too particular.' Grunfeld grinned. 'Anyway, Baron or not, Mannering's a sight too dangerous to have around. We don't want to have to leave Battersea if we can help it, and we'd have to if he was still nosing. You've done very well, Minx, very well. Now get along after Mannering.'

'What about Garston?' Minx asked.

'I'll handle Garston.' Grunfeld gripped Minx's arm tightly and pulled her close to him. 'Not feeling soft for Matthew, are you? Not forgetting who you belong to, eh?' So sure of her was he that he turned away without waiting for an answer.

Minx walked through a side entrance which led to York Road. Her M.G. was parked not far away, and soon merged into the stream of traffic going over Westminster Bridge.

Grunfeld stood for some seconds, his square features set and his eyes brutal and calculating.

'Get someone over to Brook Street, and if Mannering goes out, turn the place right over. If Mannering's the Baron he may know about those stars. He might even have them. Anyhow, that woman he runs around with, Fauntley's daughter, probably knows the truth. This is going to mean a lot of money, Legrand, a lot of money – I can see it coming.'

'*If* he's the Baron,' Legrand said.

* * *

Mannering had been at Brook Street for an hour, turning over the chances of a raid on 18 Lorler Drive. He would want to explore the house and the neighbourhood before he made the attempt, and that had to be done before dusk. He had two hours of daylight for the first survey, but before he started on it he wanted to try to get the other angles in their right perspective.

Apart from Legrand and Minx no one who worked for Grunfeld was likely to be able to outwit him. It was difficult to believe that Legrand worked on his own against Grunfeld. That left Minx.

Mannering did not think she had much love for Grunfeld. Could she have the stars?

If I could talk with her for half-an-hour, he thought, I might get somewhere, but that's no easier than getting to Lambeth. Lorler Drive's the one thing left.

Five minutes later he opened the front door, with his left hand about the gun in his pocket, for he looked on every caller as a potential envoy from Grunfeld, and was taking no risks.

He stepped back apace, unable to hide his expression.

'Good Lord, *Minx*!'

She smiled vividly.

'Can I come in?'

'Of course.' He stood back. 'Straight through – that's right.' He pulled an easy chair up, and she sat down. 'Your friend Lew has withdrawn the ban on snow, then?' he asked easily.

She looked startled.

'You guessed that? He'll go a *lot* too far one day, will Lew Grunfeld.'

'I hope he's done so already,' said Mannering gently, but his eyes were narrow and hard. 'I made you an offer once, Minx, and I'm still prepared to look after you if you break away from him. Could it be the reason you've called?'

Minx stared at him fixedly, then looked away.

'It could,' she said at last, and Mannering waited for her to go on, wondering how much of what she had to say would prove genuine.

Chapter 19
Error by Grunfeld

Grunfeld put his drink down sharply on the table.

'What happened? Don't hold out on me.'

'Oh, he fell for it easily enough,' Minx said lightly.

'When's he going?'

'Tonight. He's having a look round the place before dark, to see what's in store for him.'

'*Very* nice work,' grinned Grunfeld. 'What time's he calling, do you know?'

'He didn't say, don't ask for miracles. Where's Legrand?'

'Gone to see what he can find at Mannering's flat. I – *God*!' Grunfeld suddenly sprang to the door. 'If Legrand lifts any tools Mannering wants tonight, Mannering'll smell a rat. Get after Legrand, quick. He's in a Morris 12 somewhere in Brook Street. Tell him – '

Grunfeld was shouting, but Minx realising the dangers of that mistake had reached the door before he stopped.

She drove furiously back to Brook Street, and as the M.G. turned the corner she met Legrand, starting off in the opposite direction. She hooted sharply, and leapt from her car as Legrand pulled into the kerb.

'What is it, Minx?'

'Have you been there?'

'Yes, *and* got his stuff. He's the Baron all right.' For once Legrand showed satisfaction. 'There's no – '

'Put the stuff back,' snapped Minx. 'He'll scent a trick if it's missing; Grunfeld didn't think.'

'*Parbleu!* Of course, I – '

Legrand became almost incoherent as he realised the mistake that had been made. He snatched a small suitcase from the back of the Morris, but as he turned he saw that Mannering was entering the door to the flats.

Legrand could not go back. The mistake could not be rectified.

* * *

It was impossible for Mannering to be sure whether Minx had been wholly genuine. Her hatred of Grunfeld – so freely expressed – could have been assumed. On the other hand, she had reason enough for it. Had she not been a cocaine addict he would have felt more confident of judging her sincerity, but from an addict nothing was predictable.

In any case, he was going to Battersea.

If she had told him the truth her visit would prove a big help.

If she had lied?

Mannering accepted the added danger. There was always a counter to any trick, and he believed he could outwit Grunfeld, while also making sure whether Minx had been genuine or not. It would mean disclosing her visit – but if she had been sincere then she would be out of London by now, and away from Grunfeld's influence.

As he turned into Piccadilly, Mannering caught sight of Detective-Sergeant Tanker Tring. Tring might be on an ordinary mission, but on the other hand could easily be on his way to Brook Street with a message from Bristow. It would be better, Mannering thought, to postpone his visit to Battersea.

Three minutes after he returned Tring rang the front door bell. Mr Mannering had made a statement about his chase after the assailment of Sir David Ffoulkes which he had not signed. Would he be good enough to do so now?

Mannering read the statement, signed it, agreed with Tring that it was a bad business, and ushered the sergeant out. It was as he closed the door that he noticed the slight scratch on the varnished paintwork close to the Yale lock.

He examined the lock more closely; and he knew that it had been forced.

It was not the first time his flat had been burgled; police, and pliers of less lawful trades, had visited him by stealth in the past, always with the same object – to find evidence of the Baron. He did not believe Bristow would try to do so in this affair, and he stepped away from the door thoughtfully, with Grunfeld in his mind.

If Grunfeld was responsible, the break-in was remarkably close upon the footsteps of Minx.

Who had been here?

Cautiously, with a hand about his gun, he examined every room in the flat but all were blandly empty, showing no sign or evidence of unlawful occupation.

At last he unfastened the bureau where he kept a tool-kit and other equipment for his night escapades. There was nothing he would put beyond Grunfeld, and it flashed through his mind that an explosive might be here, a time-bomb or one to operate by concussion. Steeling himself – for there are some kinds of dangers that cannot be side-tracked, but must be met squarely – he pulled out the false drawer. The drawer was empty. There was nothing left of the tool-kit, his blue scarf, his gas-pistol and reserves of ether gas.

With cold horror he stared at the bare wood of the drawer. Every damned thing's gone, he thought. It can't be the police, they'd have waited for me, but –

The danger showed plainly, there was no sense in ignoring it. Someone had stolen the Baron's equipment from the flat of John Mannering, someone who would now have proof enough that he *was* the Baron. Proof that could be used by the police or others –

He stood up slowly, walked into the living-room and helped himself to a stiff peg of whisky. His mind was numbed with the shock of the discovery, the menace that it brought, and he cursed himself bitterly for leaving the equipment at the flat. He had taken a faint chance, and was likely to pay for it.

There was other equipment, of course; he was not worried by the loss itself. The fact that someone had it, at that moment, was the one thing of importance.

Who?

The theft had been made after he had left the flat, little more than half-an-hour ago; that seemed certain, for he would have noticed the scratch on the door when admitting Minx, or showing her out. It meant a second caller soon after Minx had gone, and it made him ponder her visit even more.

She had told him of the staff arrangements at Battersea, explained the wiring arrangements, and told him where to find Grunfeld's study on the first floor.

But whether Minx had been genuine or not, the acuteness of his danger remained.

At any moment of the night or day he might be confronted with the missing equipment, could be called on to account for it, forced to take a directed course of action to get it back. In someone's hands was a weapon for blackmail too strong even for Mannering to resist. It was a bleak, even devastating prospect, pushing every issue but the personal one aside for the time being.

Frowning, he lifted the telephone, calling the 'Greenfield' number. An unfamiliar voice answered him, to say that Mr Greenfield was out.

'Can you give him a message?' asked Mannering.

'I can't be sure when he'll receive it, sir.'

'Try and make it quickly. Tell him' – he hesitated – 'tell him that the stars will be shining tonight. Is that quite clear?'

'The stars will be shining tonight, yes, sir.'

'And ask him to be at the house for a telephone call at eight o'clock, and nine.'

Mannering rang off before the other could speak. It was then just past seven, and he did not feel that he could sit and do nothing in the flat until eight o'clock. He went out, turned towards Park Lane and, after making sure that he was not followed, entered Fuller Mansions.

As he opened the door of the flat, a movement, so slight that it might have been imaginary, caught his attention. He dropped his hand into his pocket, but before he could grip his gun a man appeared in the doorway leading to the bedroom, and in the man's hand was an automatic which pointed steadily towards his stomach.

It was Duval, poised and dangerous, and staring at a man who to him was a complete stranger.

Chapter 20
Mannering Makes a Call

It might have proved the last straw for Mannering, but instead it released the pent-up feeling he had felt since his discovery of the theft from the flat. He held back a burst of laughter.

'Come into this room,' said Duval evenly. 'Keep your hands high.' As Mannering passed him the Frenchman slipped his hand into his pocket and extracted the automatic. 'So, you come armed. Who are you?'

'That doesn't matter,' said Mannering, intent now on discovering why Duval had forced an entry and how far he could be trusted.

'It matters much,' said Duval coldly. 'The flat is of a friend of mine. You will wait until that friend arrives.'

'Nonsense, I – '

'*M'sieu*, if you are a friend of my friend that satisfies me, but until – '

'Really, Duval,' said Mannering in the testy voice of Mr Moore, 'what about a cup of coffee?'

The expression on the Frenchman's face was ludicrous. He dropped his gun-hand, his eyes widening in incredulous amazement.

'*Nom d'un nom*, it is *you !*'

'The Baron,' said Mannering cheerfully. 'What made you break in?'

'*M'sieu*, I – ' Duval sat heavily on the edge of the bed. 'It is impossible, you cannot be – but then, it happens! I – I come to report that I could not bring the man who recommended me to Garston. It was important I see you, and I decided to wait. The shock when you entered and it was not you – *par Dieu*, how many of you are there, *M'sieu*?'

'We come and go,' chuckled Mannering. 'A Baron here, a John Mannering there, and sometimes a Mr Moore.'

'Ah, *M'sieu*, I address you all. I learn that Garston is not liked, and when he asked for a man – *Tiens*! They think of me, ready for any risk. I learn, too, that Garston had sent for a helper only a short while before I am told.'

Mannering frowned.

'One thing, *M'sieu*. This afternoon, I go to the house in Battersea, of which Garston tells you. I see coming from there, quite late, the *mam'selle* whose photograph you find in Garston's wallet. It is of interest, yes?'

'Indeed it is,' said Mannering grimly, 'but not altogether surprising. I, too, have been honoured with a visit.'

'So. She is drugged, that one. Do not trust her,' said Duval sharply. 'For she goes, *M'sieu*, with the little man whose eyes are black, Legrand.'

'Together, were they? What time was this?'

'Eighteen o'clock, *M'sieu*, as you would say about six.'

'Not long before she visited me,' reflected Mannering. 'I – Duval!'

'*M'sieu?*'

'Are you with me all the way?'

'I am here to assist you, *M'sieu*, in every way it can be arranged. I do not forget easily that but for you I should now be very dead. Heaven was good to me,' said Duval with his eyes gleaming, 'for I still love the world, *M'sieu le Baron*. You had some idea in mind?'

'I had,' said Mannering softly. 'I'm going to visit Battersea, Duval, at eight o'clock, but it's not a journey I'd like to make alone. You'll follow me there, and wait outside. We'll have that scar covered – get your coat off, we haven't much time.'

Half-an-hour later, Duval's complexion had been cleverly altered. Mannering had obtained a peaked cap and coat from a theatrical costumier, and hired a Talbot – a car popular with the road police – from a garage where he was well known.

The instructions he gave Duval were clear and concise.

'I'll drive as far as Clapham Common, and you'll put the clothes on there. Then you'll take me to 18 Lorler Drive. With luck Grunfeld will come to the house while we're waiting. I'll go in to talk to him, and the fact that a police-car is outside should restrain any foolish impulses he might have. Afterwards, I'll try to come out alone, but I may be with Grunfeld. In any case, you'll be near enough at hand to follow him – understood?'

'Will you not need to come to the car, *M'sieu?*'

'If I'm out first, we'll park the car out of sight. If we come together I'll join you, you'll get out of those clothes and slip from the car soon afterwards. Follow Grunfeld, that's the one thing that matters. Quite clear, Duval?'

'I have been wishing to meet Grunfeld,' said Duval softly. 'It will be a pleasure.'

*   *   *

The hands of Mannering's wrist-watch pointed to eight precisely as he stepped from the Talbot and walked across the wide road to Number 18, Lorler Drive.

For ten minutes he had been waiting within sight of the house, but he had not seen Grunfeld. The man might have reached Number 18 earlier, of course, or might not have received the message. One thing was quite certain: talk of the stars would bring him from Lambeth in a hurry.

A man in dark clothes, and with the traditional servant's manner, opened the door.

Passing through the hall and up the stairs, Mannering looked about him. What Minx had told him of the lay-out of the house was, as far as he was able to see, quite accurate. Had his suspicions of her been justified?

'All right,' he said as the manservant stopped outside a closed door, 'you needn't announce me.' He nodded abruptly as he turned the handle of the door.

He saw Grunfeld sitting at a carved mahogany desk, in a room pleasantly, even luxuriously furnished. He would not have recognised the man but for the peculiar lightness of his eyes. For 'Mr Greenfield' wore a wig that was almost white, and affected clothes of a rich, but outmoded style.

He had a telephone in one hand, and Mannering had heard his unmistakable voice:

'I'll speak to you as soon as I know, we might have to move fast.'

And then the interruption.

Grunfeld stared across the room, his body rigid, the telephone some inches from his mouth.

Very slowly he replaced the receiver, without moving his eyes from Mannering's face.

'What – what are you doing here, Mannering?'

'Before you do anything rash, you'll be well-advised to look out of the window,' Mannering suggested pleasantly.

As one compelled against his will, Grunfeld obeyed. He had received a shock as great as any he had given, but when he saw the car and the man at the wheel, he whirled round, the savagery on his face mocking his disguise.

'You damned swine, you promised – '

'He doesn't know why I'm calling,' said Mannering, 'he's there only as a precaution, and his car carries a radio-transmitter. Just for your information, Grunfeld.'

Grunfeld sat slowly in his chair, making a patent effort to regain his self-control. He succeeded partly, and his voice took on a more confident note, almost one of bluster.

'That might seem clever, Mannering, but I wonder if he knows what I know?'

'Not all of it, or you'd be at Brixton,' said Mannering shortly.

Grunfeld hesitated, lit a cigarette, and stubbed it out before he spoke again. His nerve had been jarred by Mannering's entry, something of his complacency and confidence had suffered with it. Only temporarily, Mannering knew, for after this little setback the man would be even more dangerous.

'Look here, Mannering, we don't have to beat about the bush. I sent a man to your flat this afternoon, and he got some interesting stuff – *very* interesting stuff.'

Mannering said: 'Thanks, Grunfeld, that's what I came to learn.'

Grunfeld laughed.

'If you think again, it's *I* who should threaten *you*, Mannering. The police would be only too glad to get the Baron's insignia. Of all the damned nerve, bringing a policeman here to cover you!'

Mannering said easily: 'What you think you know and what are facts are two different things, Grunfeld, but here's one you can't alter. If I call that man in and tell him where I last saw you, you'll be in jail within half-an-hour.'

'And how far away from me would *you* be?'

'Well – I've considered that,' admitted Mannering. 'Let's look at it frankly. Legrand, wanted for two murders in Paris, could state on oath that he'd taken the Baron's gear from my flat, but it's not an oath that an English jury would accept readily. And of course I would suggest that it was an effort to discredit my evidence about Lambeth. Stalemate, I think.'

Grunfeld swallowed with difficulty.

'Supposing it is? Damn it, you wouldn't dare risk a rumour getting around that you're the Baron.'

'But I might chance it, in certain circumstances. However, there's something else, Grunfeld.' He paused, and then said sharply: 'Minx is a good actress, but the plot was poor. You damned fool, do you think I'd come *here* after you'd sent a transparent bait like that?'

Grunfeld seemed to sag.

Mannering knew in that moment that Minx *had* been sent to make sure he visited Battersea, knew that the first two objects of his visit had succeeded. Inwardly he felt a rising excitement, knowing that he had Grunfeld on the run, believing that – with care – he could finish the affair before many hours elapsed. But always in front of his mind must be the fact that Legrand and Grunfeld could testify to finding the Baron's equipment, and would do so, if they were pushed into a corner.

Yet there was Vincenne's death to avenge.

'But we're beating about the bush,' Mannering went on with a show of reason. 'We've got each other cornered, up to a point. And if we're not careful we're going to cut each other's throats. As Mannering I couldn't join you, but –'

Grunfeld stared, his fingers clenching.

'But what?'

'As the Baron I want those stars,' said Mannering gently. 'I wanted the stars from Vincenne, I was prepared to pay for them, and I'll go fifty-fifty with you now. Expenses of finding them, or paying for them, I'm not much worried either way. How does it seem?'

He eyed the other squarely as he spoke. Grunfeld was trying to acclimatise himself to the new conditions, and for a moment his eyes held an expression so cunning that Mannering knew some trickery had passed through his mind. And then he straightened up in his chair, hitching it forward.

'Ah, now you're talking, Mannering. So you're as anxious as that to get the stars, are you?'

'I am.' Mannering kept a poker-face, but felt inwardly elated. He had been sure that Grunfeld did not know where the stars were, but he imagined he would get confirmation now, one way or the other.

'All right,' Grunfeld said abruptly, 'you can rely on me letting you know if I lay my hands on them – Baron.'

'Make sure,' said Mannering gently, 'that you don't let too many other people hear that name. I'm not going to let the truth get out without a fight, Grunfeld, and although I'd stick at murdering some people my conscience wouldn't be troubled overmuch at murdering you. All this since we're being frank,' he added sardonically.

He did not offer to shake hands, and Grunfeld did not appear to expect it. Mannering went out, joined Duval, and the Talbot started off.

At the turning into the main road Duval hesitated.

'Do I wait here?'

'Yes – get a taxi if it's possible, I doubt whether he'll walk. I should have brought two cars –'

'Even the Baron cannot think of all things, M'sieu, but there is a taxi coming this way, it is all right. Your visit was successful?'

Mannering smiled gently.

'Grunfeld is now quite certain that I shall not visit him tonight, yes.'

'So?'

'I shall be there,' said Mannering.

'I am not surprised,' said Duval. 'But be advised, M'sieu, two people can play tricks. I shall report to Fuller Mansions, M'sieu, by letter if not in person. And for your gun, perhaps you will exchange a key that I need not break in?'

Mannering handed one over, and was still chuckling as he drove off, leaving Duval to talk with a taxi-driver who had pulled in at his signal.

Meanwhile, Grunfeld was saying to Legrand:

'Yes, he's the Baron all right. But we'll lay off him for a day or two, Legrand. You needn't alter anything at the house, though.'

'Why the delay?' Legrand asked disapprovingly.

'Why?' Grunfeld chuckled. 'Because he can do one or two jobs for us, can't he? If any man in England can find the stars the Baron can. He won't come to Battersea, he was too fly for that, but if he does he'll get a nasty shock. However, we don't want him dead just yet.'

They were driven from Battersea to Lambeth, and it was not until they neared the end of the journey that Grunfeld asked suddenly:

'Where's the Vincenne girl? Still at Shere?'

'There will be word of that when we get to the warehouse,' Legrand said.

There was word.

As they went down in the lift Legrand read it, and before they had reached the second floor and the room where Matthew Garston was waiting in terror for the man who had sent for him soon after Minx's visit, Legrand snapped:

'She has gone, she has left Shere!'

'Gone? Where, man, where?'

'Again it is Mannering – that infernal busybody – we have to thank for this. She is with Lorna Fauntley at the Fauntleys' house in Hampshire. Two men have followed them, men brought by Mannering.'

Grunfeld rubbed his lower lip.

'Don't worry, we'll look after her soon enough, Legrand, and' – his voice lowered, but his eyes were glittering – 'we could make even more sure of Mannering if we got the Fauntley woman as well. Could you manage that?'

'It would appear easy. The house is isolated, according to the report.'

Grunfeld grunted. That was one thing accomplished. There was yet another to be done.

Fifteen minutes later Garston's body was tied inside a weighted sack and prepared for dropping into the Thames, while Grunfeld, grim-faced and savage, sought out Legrand.

'Get those women,' he said abruptly.

Legrand eyed him curiously.

'You know of the stars?'

'I reckon there's a hell of a lot of funny business going on I'm not standing for,' snapped Grunfeld. 'I want those women – and Mannering. Get busy, Legrand, there isn't much time.'

The stars of Louis would not be at 18 Lorler Drive, but possibly he would find the stolen equipment, for Mannering had no intention of trusting Grunfeld. It was a case of wits against wits, and probably death at the end of it for one or the other.

In no spirit of bravado he prepared for the raid, and he was halfway through his disguise when Duval came to Fuller Mansions. The Frenchman showed every sign of frustration and despair.

'I lose him, *M'sieu*, I follow to Lambeth, past the bridge, he turns right, and there – *tiens*, it is a city this London, the same road it leads everywhere! I cannot blame myself enough, he escapes me, and – '

'I'll get a car for you,' Mannering consoled him, 'and you can watch 18 Lorler Drive – *after* tonight, for tonight I'm going alone.'

'It is my opinion,' said Duval gravely, 'that *M'sieu* will not die on his back.'

And Mannering laughed.

But he was not laughing when he turned into Lorler Drive.

He had turned his car into the gates of a house three removed from Number 18, leaving the nose pointing towards the street for a quick getaway if the need arose.

Both Garston and Minx had said the house he aimed to burgle was often empty. It looked empty.

As he slipped into the driveway, he wondered just what kind of reception Grunfeld would have planned.

He walked to the front door and rang the bell.

There was no answer, and he tried again. Darkness and silence answered him, and his conviction that the place was empty grew apace. The front windows were too close to a street lamp to work on with safety, and he turned to the back. Here he found one with shutters on the outside, French fashion. The screws which held them in position offered little resistance, and within ten minutes he had lifted one shutter out of its place.

As he picked up his diamond cutter, Mannering knew that he was faced with a challenge that could not have been stronger. Every known prevention against burglary would be here, legal and illegal; that much was certain.

Expertly he ran the cutter round the whole area of the window which was some five feet high by two across. When at last he drew the glass gently from its framework, he saw that he was little nearer the room, for shutters on the inside presented an uncompromising barrier. Deftly he drew a pair of asbestos-tipped rubber gloves and a small coil of wire from his kit; the wire was connected with a small portable battery, for he had come prepared to test the efficiency of Grunfeld's electric safeguards. He touched the wire quickly against the shutters, and a vivid blue spark dazzled his eyes. He tried again, with the same result.

'*A la* Garston,' he muttered, and shone his torch round the inner shutters. It would be impossible to force them back with the current on; they would have to be cut.

The danger of this undertaking would be from the constant light which might attract attention, but he had prepared for that. A piece of rubberised cloth, through slits in which he inserted his hands, kept the flame confined to a small space.

The shutter was made of sheet steel, and the cutter went through it easily and quickly. As he severed the last shred of the second lock the shutters sagged, and the Baron drew back, well-satisfied. Collecting his tools, he stepped through into a room which the moonlight revealed as a small library. He went straight to the door, tried it, and found it locked on the outside. This presented little difficulty, and after a few minutes work on it he opened the door cautiously and found himself in the hall through which he had entered earlier that night.

Grunfeld's study was his main objective.

Thick carpet muffled his footsteps as he hurried up the stairs, keeping the pencil of light shining downwards slightly ahead of him. He could hear the slow *tick-tock* of a clock echoing with a sharp precision, growing louder as he approached the study door. His hand was on the handle when the clock struck one, a deep note so penetrating and un-expected that it made him swing round, sending his heart to his mouth.

He steadied, laughed at himself, and yet remained uneasy.

The house was empty, there was little or no risk, and now that he was inside there should prove no serious emergency ahead; yet a premonition of danger remained.

Had it been too easy?

He pushed that thought aside; the forced entry had been a job of which the Baron at his heyday could be proud. And yet –

He tried the study handle, still wearing the rubber gloves. The door was locked, of course. He started to draw his gloves off, stopped, and touched the battery set coil against the door knob.

A vivid blue flame lit up the landing, the door, the hanging pictures. He snatched his hand away, conscious of a sharp burning pain in his eyes. He stood there swaying, not daring to lean against the wall for fear that that, too, was alive with current.

Gradually his sight returned, but ten minutes passed before he felt well enough to return to the attack on the study with any confidence.

This place was alive with electricity.

Why was it necessary?

What did Grunfeld keep here?

These questions in the forefront of his mind, he realised that the best means of getting by without further danger was to find the electric-power switch. He moved away from the study, and found that the doors leading to the domestic quarters were locked but not electrified. He looked for a cellar door, and found one leading from a small pantry near the kitchen.

In another ten seconds he knew that he had found the entry of the power-house.

It was immediately ahead of him at the foot of the cellar stairs, a tall barred door bearing a red-lettered card of warning.

He looked upwards towards the ceiling, and saw the steel conduit containing the cables passing through a hole at the top of the power-house wall. He knew that he had only to cut them to break down the whole system.

Cut them? There was a quicker, less dangerous way.

He took a small stick of dynamite from his tool-kit, and fixed it between the conduit and the ceiling. A foot of fuse dangled down from it, and he struck a match, watched until the fuse spluttered, and retreated quickly up the stairs.

In three minutes a faint 'boom' came to his ears.

He waited for another minute to pass before opening the cellar door. Fumes drifted into his face, thick and nauseating. It was some minutes before he was able to see the broken conduit and the torn wires, but then he knew that there would be no further need to fear the current; the house was at his mercy.

He worked hard on the lock of the study door, using first one and then another of his highly specialised tools. At last the door swung open.

He stepped through –

And stopped, alarm shearing through him.

Something was touching his head and shoulders, running down his clothes, into his eyes, his ears, his mouth. He was filled for a moment with a fierce, overwhelming panic, for some liquid had been put above the door to drench an intruder.

Acid –

He forced himself to stand still, shone the torch towards the floor, and saw then what it was.

Water, coming down in a fine spray, put into action by the opening of the door.

He knew what reception had been planned, then.

Had he taken Minx's bait he would have been allowed to get into the study; the water would have poured over him, and then, *only* then, the current would have been switched on, and anything he had touched would have killed him on the instant.

*   *   *

There was a cold hatred in Mannering's mind for the men who had planned that thing.

Grunfeld, Minx and Legrand had all been a party to it.

He dried himself as best he could and then turned to the wall-safe. It took him twenty minutes to cut through, and was disappointingly empty. He gathered up the few papers it contained, however, still wondering why Grunfeld kept the place so guarded.

Among the papers was a small packet wrapped in brown paper, and it was this which gave Mannering the most likely explanation. He opened it slowly, the idea even then in his mind, and he saw a fine white powder.

Mannering saw everything, then; he seemed to know it with an unquestioning certainty; every mystery of Grunfeld, Legrand and Garston was explained, except their interest in the stars of Louis.

To Mannering at that moment the stars were unimportant.

If he was right, there would be cocaine in the house in sufficient quantities to make Grunfeld go to any lengths to prevent it being found.

He started a search of the study, tapping the walls, opening every piece of furniture, failing to find what he wanted but fully convinced it was at hand. When he found it, a store of cocaine that would supply the London demand for months, it was beneath the floor. Only the surrounds were of steel, the centre was of wooden boarding; beneath that was packet after packet of cocaine, each at least a pound in weight.

Chapter 22
Quick Change

It was after five o'clock when Mr Moore slipped into the Fuller Mansions flat, to find Duval awaiting him with coffee. Told the essentials, his face lost its look of expectant welcome and became grim and forbidding.

'So, drugs, *M'sieu*. Murder with a knife is better. It is a big ugliness you have discovered, but – how will you prevent it continuing? That must be done.'

Mannering leaned back with his eyes closed.

'You are right, it must be done, Duval. I'll have to find a way. If needs be the police will have to act.'

'Even though Grunfeld knows of the Baron?'

Mannering murmured: 'I wonder how many drug victims there are in London, Duval? A thousand? Five thousand?'

'It is so, *M'sieu*, you are right. And for this, I can imagine the police will wink many eyes. But *M'sieu* will be well advised to sleep, and afterwards it will be easier to think.'

Mannering turned in without another word, and slept until it was nearly noon. Bathed, dressed, a light breakfast finished, he reviewed the situation with a dispassionate regard.

The police would have to be told, of course, it was a discovery which Mannering could not keep to himself. There remained his own problem: how to get back the Baron's stolen equipment from Grunfeld, and prevent the story being given to the Yard.

He held the trump card, yet against his knowledge of Grunfeld's fuller activities there was the continued disappearance of the four stars of Louis, and the threat to himself. Stalemate for the time being; but the issue would have to be forced soon. Grunfeld would move without wasting much time.

Mannering gathered up the papers he had removed from Grunfeld's safe and walked with Duval from Park Lane to Brook Street, stopping on the way to deposit the parcel at his bank.

Duval had not been to Brook Street before, and as he turned with Mannering towards the flat he stopped abruptly, staring at a Renault drawn up at the kerb.

'The driver, *M'sieur*,' he muttered in a quick undertone, 'a man it is not comfortable for me to meet.'

The driver stepped from the car and went importantly into the entrance.

Inspector Bon, of the *Sûreté* – calling on Mannering!

Mannering said quickly: 'Get back to Fuller Mansions, Duval. I'll send for you when the coast is clear.'

The Frenchman turned at once, and Mannering went on alone, wondering what purpose Bon had in calling. He hurried upstairs by the lift, arriving at the door of his flat as Bon was ringing the bell.

'Good morning, Inspector –'

Bon swung round.

'So, here you are, *M'sieu* Mannering! I come in a great hurry to see you. How soon can we talk, please?'

'I'm at your service.' Mannering inserted a key in the lock, and led the way in.

'You wonder why I wish to see you, *M'sieu*? It is of the young daughter of Raoul Vincenne I speak. I, Bon, would talk with her, it is possible she knows more of the stars of Louis than she admits to the English police, but – pouf? – she has gone.' An expression of resignation crossed Bon's face, and he spread his hands.

Mannering's heart beat quickly: this call was neither accidental nor without guile. Had the Yard, or Bon, learned where Annette was?

'So,' said Bon, with a great show of innocence, '*M'sieu* Bristow, he advise *you* might know where to find that foolish girl.'

Mannering raised his eyebrows.

'An odd thing to suggest, Bon. Why should I?'

'*M'sieu* – not so odd.' A stubby forefinger pointed towards Mannering. 'The stars of Louis must be recovered. I, Bon, can stop at nothing to find them. And – *you* do not speak all the truth, that I know.'

Mannering's expression hardened, his voice grew sharp.

'I don't like your attitude, Bon, and –'

'*M'sieu*! Yesterday it is learned that you visit Annette Vincenne at a hotel in Surrey, yes. Clayton, he has admitted that, but will not say to Bristow where she has gone, he says he does not know. *You* know, *M'sieu*, and –'

Brrr-brrr!

The telephone cut across Bon's words. Mannering lifted the instrument with a muttered apology, trying to think of a way of answering Bon without implicating himself too deeply.

'Mannering speaking, who is that?'

It was Grunfeld's voice that answered him. In it was packed a savagery that appalled him. Strangled, venomous, the words came over the wire.

'I've got you just where I want you, and by God you'll pay for last night's work! Think you put one over me, didn't you? Well, listen Mannering, if you put the police on to that place you say goodbye to the Vincenne girl *and* Lorna Fauntley. Legrand picked them up early this morning, and here they stay until I've got you. Try and work that out!'

The receiver at the other end banged down.

Mannering stood, staring at the wall. His face had lost most of its colour, and his eyes were bleak, his expression one of sheer despair. How long he stayed like that he did not know. It was Bon who interrupted him, and there was a sharp, apprehensive note in the Frenchman's voice.

'Mannering! What –'

The tension broke.

Mannering turned his head, regarded Bon sombrely, and replaced the receiver. He said evenly:

'I don't know where Annette Vincenne is, Bon, and you can tell Bristow that. You can also tell him to cram Lambeth, roads and river, with his men by four o'clock this afternoon, because between then and midnight there is going to be trouble. And you can tell him that some time today he'll have a message explaining more clearly, and the message won't be sent for fun. Clear?'

'*M'sieu*, it is difficult –'

'It needn't be. If I knew where Annette was I'd tell you, by God, I'd tell you! If you ever want to see her alive again just go back to the Yard and give my message to Bristow.'

There was a pause, while Bon stared at the gaunt face in front of him; and then he shrugged his shoulders and went out.

Chapter 23
Surrender?

He had no idea where to find Grunfeld, except that it was somewhere in Lambeth, and he did not believe that he or the police would be able to locate that apartment unaided. He could tell Bristow to send men to follow him when he left the flat with Grunfeld's envoy – but the police would be seen. That was virtually certain, Mannering thought, for in this *finale* Grunfeld would take no risks. Even if the faint chance did succeed, once the police reached the outer entrance to the apartment they would have the electrically-controlled doors to break down, which would take time. With Grunfeld and Legrand inside, as well as the two girls and himself, there was little doubt of what would happen.

And Grunfeld had a way out, to the river.

The only prospect was cold murder; of himself, Lorna, and Annette.

Even if he surrendered without telling the police or sending a fuller message, he was fairly sure Lorna would not be released.

Could it mean complete surrender?

If there was no hope for himself or Lorna, except the remote possibility that she would be exchanged for him, what object was there in keeping anything back from Bristow?

He stood up abruptly, and went to his writing-bureau. He wrote quickly, blotted what he had written, sealed it in an envelope and then telephoned Fuller Mansions. Duval answered.

'Duval, listen carefully. Come at once to Brook Street, in a taxi, and watch my flat. Legrand or Grunfeld will call, but you're to do nothing. I shall go out with them.'

'*M'sieu*, what – ' Duval was alarmed.

Mannering went on as though there had been no interruption.

'As soon as I am out of sight, go into the flat and take an envelope from beneath the main bedroom carpet. Is that clear?'

'Yes, *M'sieu.*'

'I shall leave a key with the porter here, and tell him you're going to call for it. Take the letter and see that it is delivered to Inspector Bristow at Scotland Yard, just two hours after I have left. Neither more nor less, is that clear?'

'But yes, *M'sieu.* You – you sound as if there is bad news. Is there no way I can help?'

'Only by doing what I ask you. By the time the letter is delivered, I expect to be in the Lambeth area.'

'I – I comprehend, *M'sieu*, it will be done.'

'Thanks,' said Mannering slowly.

He put the letter beneath the carpet, and then went down-stairs and left a key of his flat with the porter. He described Duval to make sure there would be no mistake. Then he went into the bathroom, and mixed a couple of powders very carefully. He scooped the mixture into a small envelope which he placed in a box and slipped into his pocket. That finished he went back to the living-room and waited.

Legrand and the other man came at two o'clock.

*　　*　　*

'From here,' said Legrand softly, 'we shall go to your bank, *M'sieu*, and your safe-deposit, and withdraw what valuables you keep there, and what money you can take without causing surprise. Also the papers you took last night. Before, you will collect any jewels which you may have in this flat, and hand them to me. I warn you to be very quick and attempt no subterfuge.'

Mannering looked at Legrand coldly and without fear. It put a slight, a very slight, constraint on his captors.

There was little of value at the flat: two small diamond pieces which he had bought a few days before but not taken to his safe-deposit, and a hundred pounds in treasury notes. Legrand made no comment, and they drove from Brook Street to his bank, where Mannering went in alone, cashed a cheque for a thousand pounds and collected the packet of papers. From Fuller Mansions he obtained the other documents.

The safe-deposit was a different matter.

His was in the Haymarket, and in the case which he drew out were jewels worth a hundred thousand pounds, part of his collection which, although small, was intrinsically invaluable.

That done, they allowed him to smoke, but for the rest of the journey Mannering was compelled to wear the dark glasses he had worn before.

In little more than ten minutes the car pulled up, and he was helped out. As his feet touched the pavement he dropped a matchbox. He heard the faint click as it reached the ground, but there was no pause from Legrand or his companion, and he was hustled into the building and on to the underground lounge where Grunfeld waited, smiling unpleasantly.

'Another social call, Mannering? A whisky, or would you prefer coffee again?'

'Nice of you,' said Mannering, 'but nothing just now, thanks, later will do.'

'Later? Ah me! I greatly fear there won't be any later for you. Mannering and the Baron in one go, *that* ought to please the police! How much did he bring with him, Legrand?'

Legrand handed over the brief-case, and Grunfeld went through the contents, letting the jewels run through his fingers as if he could barely let them go.

Mannering said pleasantly: 'A pity there isn't a drug to cure greed, Grunfeld, it might be some use to you.'

'When I want you to talk I'll tell you!' snarled Grunfeld, and before Mannering knew what he was going to do he stepped sharply across the room and brought his palm against Mannering's face. The blow stung, and Mannering staggered back, but the only reaction he showed was the contempt in his eyes. Grunfeld drew back, his lips curling.

'Where are the stars?'

'I don't know.'

'Don't lie to me! Where are they?'

'I don't know.'

'Legrand –'

The little Frenchman was on his feet at once. He stepped softly to Mannering, gripped his right wrist and forced Mannering's arm behind him into a half-Nelson. Agony shot through Mannering's arm and shoulder; he gasped convulsively, and then tightened his lips. The pain increased, it seemed that something must break; sweat beaded his forehead and his face lost its colour. But his eyes did not move from Grunfeld's.

'All right,' Grunfeld snapped. 'So you don't know. Clever chap, aren't you? *Miss* Fauntley and the French kid relied on you, didn't they? Well, I'm looking after them now. Couldn't guess how, could you?'

Mannering said evenly: 'Supposing you tell me.'

131

'Surely I'll tell you. They're staying in London for a week, Mannering. Not here. I'm clearing out of here for a few days. I'm sure you can guess what my last job will be. It won't take long, and the place'll be empty in less than an hour.'

Mannering said: 'You were going to tell me about Miss Fauntley.'

'So I was! I'm taking them to somewhere in the country. In a month they won't be able to live without cocaine. Ever seen a friend of yours go under to that stuff, Mannering? You should do, it's quite an experience.'

Mannering did not see Grunfeld, nor Minx behind him, nor the room. He seemed to be looking through a red mist, and there was a volcano within him. He had feared murder, but this horror had not passed through his mind.

Lorna, crippled with drugs.

Physically, mentally crippled, wholly dependent on the drug, completely controlled by the supplier. It was useless to try to tell himself that her strong personality could not be subjected; he knew that no one could be proof against it.

He remembered Minx on her knees and begging for a shot. Pleading, crying, abasing herself for it.

Lorna like that –

Mannering fought down a hopelessness that threatened to unman him. The finality of Grunfeld's manner, the vicious simplicity of his plan, were alike inescapable. He said thickly.

'Why not kill her, Grunfeld?'

'That's a fine idea,' sneered Grunfeld. 'Her father's the biggest collector of jewels in England and she can get at them all right. What do you think I'm going to work on her for? And I wouldn't keep the Vincenne kid, only she's the type to attract fools, she'll earn her keep. Satisfied *now*?'

Mannering said: 'Yes, I'm satisfied.'

It was the end, as far as he could see there was no escape. Not even a remote chance of one.

And then, slowly, a glimmer of hope filtered through despair.

When Grunfeld had talked of drugging Lorna everything had been wiped from his mind, his plans, his hurried arrangements, his time-limit of two hours before Duval went to Scotland Yard. He had left the flat at two-fifteen, and from a clock set in the wall he saw that it was now nearly half-past three.

He cursed himself savagely. He had impressed the need for

132

keeping to the two-hour interval and it would prove too long. Grunfeld would be away from here, there was no chance of the police arriving in time. They would arrive; at least he had made sure of that. Legrand noticed most things, but had missed the matchbox.

Grunfeld's voice came sharply.

'What're you thinking, Mannering? Legrand, take his arm, he's got something in his mind . . . now talk, you swine, talk!' Grunfeld struck Mannering's face again, while Legrand forced up his right arm, bringing back the sudden agonising pain.

He sagged forward.

'Let him go,' snapped Grunfeld. 'He'll talk. Now what's on your mind?'

'Don't – don't do that again,' Mannering gasped. 'There is a limit to what I can stand, Grunfeld. For God's sake don't –'

'Well, let's have it. Every man has his breaking point, though I must say I thought yours would take a little longer to reach.'

Mannering muttered: 'I told – the police to go to Battersea by midnight tonight, told them about Garston's place. I thought they'd make Garston talk –'

Had the lie worked? He saw no chance of saving himself, but something might delay Grunfeld until the time-limit expired and the police came. That at least would save Lorna from the full viciousness of the plan.

Grunfeld laughed.

'Well, Garston won't talk – *can't* talk. That's very sure. Know his line I suppose?'

'I'd guessed. He distributed the – the stuff through his shops.'

'So you'd got as far as that?' Grunfeld said softly. 'You were smart, Mannering; what a pity you weren't more careful. Like to know more? We have the shipments in here, parcel it up and take it to Battersea for distribution. Simple, isn't it? We've got some other distributors, too, Minx is one of them. So you'd guessed –'

'Aren't you wasting a lot of time?' Minx put in irritably. 'Let's talk to Vincenne about the stars, we might as well find what she knows and get it over.'

Grunfeld turned on her, snarling.

'Maybe you're right. The river was the way we planned, wasn't it, Mannering? You might as well have another look at it, but you won't come up this time. Not alive.'

Ten minutes to four.

An hour at least before the police would get here. But they would never find the apartment until Bristow read the note Duval was to deliver. He would find it then –

An hour – he must gain an hour, or try to.

'Grunfeld.' His voice sharpened as Legrand came towards him and gripped his arm.

'Well, what is it?'

Mannering said slowly: 'There are things I could tell you, if there were time.'

Grunfeld said harshly: 'No stalling, Mannering. If you'd got anything worth saying you'd have put it across five minutes ago. I – '

It was then, quite suddenly and without warning, that a high-pitched buzzing sound rang through the room. It jarred on Mannering's ears, but the effect on Grunfeld and Minx was startling enough to drive all thought of pain or discomfort from his mind. Grunfeld swung towards the door, his face losing colour. Minx gasped aloud, the nerve at one corner of her mouth twitching violently.

'Who the hell's that? There *can't* be any trouble – '

Legrand had disappeared, and a moment later voices were heard, Legrand's and another, brusquer voice. One Mannering had not expected to hear again, one that came with a stupefying unexpectedness.

The door was pushed open.

'It's true, Boss. I'm telling you. There's a cordon of police round the warehouse. We're trapped!'

And even then the news he brought did not immediately come home to Mannering, for it was *young Clayton* who entered with Legrand, sharp-voiced and insolent as he had always been.

Clayton – who called Grunfeld 'Boss'!

Chapter 24
Four Stars

There was little time in which to realise the implications of Clayton's words, or to assimilate the fact that he worked for Grunfeld, but the moment remained vivid in Mannering's mind.

'I have locked everything,' Legrand was saying hoarsely, 'they can't get in.'

Grunfeld and Minx looked from one man to the next, fear in their eyes.

'You – you're sure about this, Clayton?' Grunfeld gripped the youngster's arm.

'Of course I'm sure. Every damned door is watched, and they'll be in the warehouse in five minutes. What a damned fool I was not to have cleared out while I had the chance. But there's the river passage, isn't there? We *can* make it.'

'If, as you say, we are trapped,' Legrand said, 'the river will certainly be watched.'

Minx screamed, her control gone.

'Shut up, you slut!' roared Grunfeld, pushing her away so roughly that she fell to the floor. She did not move but stayed there staring up at him, terror in her eyes. Grunfeld swung round on Mannering.

'You – '

'He can die later if it's true,' Legrand said sharply. 'Or at worst the police can have the Baron. There may be a chance left, I'll go to the river to make sure.'

'Take Mannering downstairs; I'll go,' Grunfeld said.

Legrand put a gun to the back of Mannering's neck and urged him towards the door leading to the lower floor.

'It is clever,' Legrand said impersonally. 'How did you bring them, Mannering?'

Mannering said: 'I dropped a matchbox containing some flowers of sulphur and a little dynamite. I'd tucked a cigarette end in before dropping it. It could only cause a bang, smoke and a smell that the police would learn of quickly.'

'And then?'

'The police had word to say that it would be at the entrance to the rendezvous, and to surround the place,' said Mannering. He did not add that Duval had taken a note telling Bristow of the ruse before it had been due.

'So, a simple plot, but it has worked. Now you will join the women, and if the police do break in – *allons*, it is over. This floor will be flooded – simple too, you see. If the police do not find us – ' Legrand shrugged. 'We shall get away, the women will be as Grunfeld said, and we shall have much cocaine to dry out before it can be sold.'

It was said with a quiet finality that allowed no possibility of alteration. Mannering was filled with a savage hopelessness. Death, then, for them all.

'*Legrand!*'

The name was screamed from the far end of the passage. It was Minx's voice, so distorted with terror that it was hardly recognisable.

'No, no, they mustn't take me, they – '

There was a rush of footsteps, another cry, as Minx flung herself on Legrand.

Mannering simply bent his knee, losing a foot in height, and as he did so the sharp snap of a shot from the silenced gun hissed, and he felt the bullet stir his hair. He swung round as Legrand went sprawling, overborne by Minx's insanely clinging arms.

Mannering seized the gun, conscious of no elation, no relief, only of taking what slender chance there was of averting disaster.

'Open the women's door, Legrand.'

The Frenchman hesitated, scrambled up, and went slowly forward. He unlocked a door and pushed it open. Mannering caught a glimpse of Lorna and Annette, but his attention was caught by a sudden movement from Legrand, a movement that told him the man carried a second automatic in a shoulder-holster. As Legrand's finger found the trigger of his second gun, Mannering fired. Two shots rang out simultaneously. Mannering felt a fierce pain at his shoulder as Legrand fell, dead before his body reached the floor.

Mannering stood there unsteadily, breathing hard. Lorna moved forward and put an arm about him.

'Which way, John? I'll help you get there.'

'Take – Legrand's gun,' Mannering gasped. 'Grunfeld, young Clayton and another man, up the passage. Shoot – on sight, don't give them a chance.' His strength returned in a sudden burst of anger towards Annette, who had darted back into the room. 'Come back you little fool!'

She came, carrying her handbag, her face suggesting a dozen emotions.

'I forgot this, yes. We will be all right, *M'sieu*?'

'God knows,' muttered Mannering. 'I – careful!'

She tripped, recovered, but her bag dropped to the floor and burst open.

And Mannering looked down.

Among the frivolous and pathetic oddments of a woman's handbag, something sparkled like living fire, something that had been wrapped in cotton-wool which had now fallen apart. In that moment Mannering forgot his wound, forgot the danger, as he stared down at the four missing stars of Louis, spilled from Annette's bag.

* * *

He had the stars in his pocket, and Annette was backing away from him and the gun in his hand. Her eyes glittered like a wild cat's, she was livid with fury.

'They're mine, I tell you, mine! I didn't steal them. My father would have lost them, I changed them for the others, and then when he died I – they're mine! *Give them to me!*'

Mannering said evenly: 'The police will be here in five minutes, you little fool. They're having the stars, and if you don't keep quiet they'll have you too. Understand that – prison, five or six years of it. The police are on the premises.'

'The – *police*?' She lost her rage in sudden fear.

'Yes, does that make sense?'

'I – no, no, they mustn't take me away, please don't let them, I did no wrong, I didn't mean –'

It was then they heard the explosion.

The 'boom' roared in their ears, making them reel backwards. Annette gasped in fright and clung to Lorna, and Mannering leaned against the wall, knowing the police had blown down one of the steel doors. They would not take long to get through.

He began to lead the way to the lounge.

There was one thing he had not seen before: in the wall near Grunfeld's escritoire there was a gap wide enough for a man to pass through, made by a sliding partition. From it a confused echo of sound was coming, and getting closer. He motioned

Lorna and Annette out of sight, waiting with his gun raised in his uninjured arm.

Footfalls and voices, the first one Grunfeld's.

'*You* can talk, you damned fool, the Vincenne girl had the sparklers all the time, Garston bought one from her. He –'

'I knew she was scared of the police, I tried to make her talk to Mannering, she didn't trust me all that much. But – what the hell does that matter?' shouted Clayton. The voices were much nearer, at any moment the two men would step through. 'What are you coming back for, this isn't the way to the river!'

'The river's blocked,' snarled Grunfeld.

Clayton swore – and then Grunfeld stepped through the gap. In his hand were two cases, Mannering's and his own. Greedy, even in emergency, he had not forgotten to take the jewels and the papers with him. Clayton followed, angry and frightened.

'We've got to get out, I –'

'Both of you,' said Mannering, 'can put your hands up.'

The men stopped in their tracks.

'Drop those cases,' Mannering said.

Grunfeld obeyed.

'Pick up the bigger case, Lorna, and open it, there's a paste set of the stars somewhere –'

'There – I see it, there!' exclaimed Annette excitedly.

'Put them loose in your bag. You've had them all the time, understand, *all* the time.'

'But –'

Hurried footsteps sounded outside the door. Grunfeld dropped his hand to his side, and Mannering saw him flash out a gun from his pocket.

Before Mannering could shoot, Clayton jumped in his line of vision.

The door burst open, admitting four armed policemen, Bristow and Bon in the rear. Mannering saw the stabs of flame, heard the snap of Grunfeld's silenced automatic and the roar of the heavier police revolvers.

Before the police reached him Grunfeld had turned the gun on himself with a sudden movement they could not stop. Lorna shut her eyes as Grunfeld slumped down, Annette screamed –

Mannering felt only relief, for now Clayton and Minx were

the only members of Grunfeld's party caught alive, and they could do little harm.

* * *

They had wanted to take Mannering to a private ward, but with the bullet out of his shoulder and the wound bandaged he insisted on going to Brook Street. He had his way, and made a brave attempt to sleep the clock round. A nurse tried to keep Bristow and Bon out of his room when he awakened next day, but without success. Lorna and Annette were at the flat. Duval stayed at Fuller Mansions.

It was on the third day that Mannering talked to Annette, while Lorna sat on a window-seat and listened.

'You needn't worry about the police, Annette,' Mannering said. 'I've told them I found the stars at Lambeth. They're not worried about you.'

'You – you can swear to that?'

'I can.'

'*Le bon Dieu* will thank you, *M'sieu*. It – it is most simple, yes. My father, he was so anxious to prove who he was, a direct descendant of Louis Quinze,' she added proudly. 'That can never be doubted, *M'sieu*.'

'Of course not,' Mannering said.

'And so he needed money. He told Richard of it, and was lent money. Afterwards Richard made it difficult, saying he was ruined, and – and he suggest to my father that the stars be stolen.'

Mannering stared.

'*Clayton* suggested that?'

'Who else, *M'sieu*? Would such an idea enter the head of Raoul Vincenne? Richard, he was most persuading, he would arrange the whole thing, he knew who would do it. And so it was arranged, and Richard was to receive one quarter for his help.'

'I see,' said Mannering.

Clayton, one of Grunfeld's chief distributing agents, had heard Vincenne's story and passed it to Grunfeld, who saw a chance of getting the stars and leaving Vincenne to hold them while they were 'hot'. But then:

'After, this man Grunfeld sees my father and demands more money,' said Annette. 'The morning after he was to bring the stars to you, *M'sieu* Mannering. Me, I believe my father will be robbed, I put false ones – for the Vincennes have the likeness of *all* the Louis Quinze gems, they are theirs by right! – for those that are real. I tell no one, not even Richard, although Richard calls Grunfeld many names. And then my father comes to see you, and is killed and robbed, and I am frightened – yes, *M'sieu*, there is no one I can trust. I wrap the diamonds and keep them always with me, but say I know nothing.'

And so it had been. Other things sorted themselves out with that knowledge. Grunfeld, dissatisfied with Clayton's efforts to make Annette talk, had kidnapped her; Clayton, remaining close at hand, knowing what was happening, thus near when Annette escaped from the car. Clayton, careful to make Annette believe in him, took her to Surrey and appeared to be helping all he could, while, in fact, he was reporting to Grunfeld: small wonder Grunfeld had learned where Annette had gone, and with whom she had been. And Clayton, when questioned, had told the police a half story, implicating Mannering – hence Bon's call.

'But one star was missing,' Mannering said.

Annette flushed hotly.

'*M'sieu*, I was without money, there was one man I knew would buy a diamond, very cheap. That was Garston, who my father disliked. I sold it to him for five hundred pounds.'

'So *that's* it!' exclaimed Mannering.

'I – I cannot thank you enough, *M'sieu*,' Annette whispered. 'You and Lorna.'

Mannering smiled.

'One other thing, Annette – the time you telephoned me, why was that?'

'Richard, he told me you could not be trusted, to be rid of you. That was the way I try, *M'sieu*.'

There was little left to learn, after hearing that Garston was Minx's husband. There was one thing that gave Mannering some concern, however, and that was Duval's future; on this question he talked discreetly to the ebullient Bon.

Bon looked grave.

'It is known he was mixed up in the affair, *M'sieu*, but he did not steal the stars of Louis, that also is known. *Nom d'un nom*, if such a man could find employ with a gentleman one could trust – he could desert the life of crime, *M'sieu* Mannering. I, Bon, would be happy.'

'Thank you,' smiled Mannering.

'Thanks, *M'sieu*? I do not understand. But there is one

thing I do know, and that is the gratitude of the *Sûreté*. The stars of Louis will be returned to the Louvre, but I shall send you a souvenir, if you will accept. A replica of the stars of Louis – for your collection.'

'I'll be delighted,' said Mannering warmingly, guessing, by the twinkle in Bon's eye, that it was the Baron's collection to which he referred.

There was one more call to make, and Mannering dialled the Fuller Mansions flat, to hear Duval answer:

'Yes, *M'sieu*?'

'You're now my cook-cum-valet,' said Mannering, 'it's all arranged with Bon, and I'm dying for a cup of coffee, so come quickly.'

When he replaced the receiver, to Lorna's joy he was laughing happily.

JOHN CREASEY

Here is a selection published by CORGI BOOKS

FIND THE BODY 25p (5s)
FIRST A MURDER 25p (5s)
RUN AWAY TO MURDER 25p (5s)

> These are all titles from the famous 'Folly of the Yard' series, written under the name of Jeremy Yorke.
> Folly is one of Creasey's most finely drawn characters ; he is a gentleman policeman, and a gourmet who hates any physical discomfort.

HERE IS DANGER 20p (4s)

> A Patrick Dawlish thriller. Written under the pen name Gordon Ashe.
> The story of Barney Day : one time crook and well-known London fence who decides to go straight and open an antique shop. But then there is a dead policeman. . . .

WARN THE BARON 20p (4s)

> Writing as Anthony Morton, creator of the Baron, we have a new tale featuring the most dare-devil ace cracksman in the annals of crime. The lean, Mayfair-man-about-town — John Mannering, the Baron.

See all these and other John Creasey titles in your Bookshop now!
All Published by CORGI BOOKS

A SELECTION OF FINE READING
AVAILABLE IN CORGI BOOKS

Novels

☐ 552 08351 8	TELL ME HOW LONG THE TRAIN'S BEEN GONE	James Baldwin	7/–
☐ 552 08506 5	A RAGING CALM	Stan Barstow	7/–
☐ 552 07938 3	THE NAKED LUNCH	William Burroughs	7/6
☐ 552 08465 4	THE SOFT MACHINE	William Burroughs	7/–
☐ 552 08492 1	TOBACCO ROAD	Erskine Caldwell	5/–
☐ 552 08562 6	GOD'S LITTLE ACRE	Erskine Caldwell	5/–
☐ 552 08493 X	THE LONG CORRIDOR	Catherine Cookson	5/–
☐ 552 08561 8	THE UNBAITED TRAP	Catherine Cookson	5/–
☐ 552 08183 3	BOYS AND GIRLS TOGETHER	William Goldman	7/6
☐ 552 08583 9	ACT OF LOVE	Celia Dale	6/–
☐ 552 08585 5	THE PHILANDERER	Stanley Kauffmann	6/–
☐ 552 08586 3	A DISTANT TRUMPET	Paul Horgan	10/–
☐ 552 08125 6	CATCH-22	Joseph Heller	7/–
☐ 552 08507 3	THE HERITAGE	Frances Parkinson Keyes	6/–
☐ 552 08524 3	THE KITES OF WAR	Derek Lambert	6/–
☐ 552 08650 X	BLOSSOM LIKE THE ROSE	Norah Lofts	6/–
☐ 552 08466 2	HERE WAS A MAN	Norah Lofts	6/–
☐ 552 08442 5	THE AU PAIR BOY	Andrew McCall	6/–
☐ 552 08564 2	VENUS IN PLASTIC	James Mitchell	4/–
☐ 552 08002 0	MY SISTER, MY BRIDE	Edwina Mark	5/–
☐ 552 08467 0	ALMOST AN AFFAIR	Nan Maynard	6/–
☐ 552 08502 2	CARAVANS	James A. Michener	5/–
☐ 552 08124 9	LOLITA	Vladimir Nabokov	6/–
☐ 552 08525 1	THE MARIGOLD FIELD	Diane Pearson	6/–
☐ 552 08491 3	PRETTY MAIDS ALL IN A ROW	Francis Pollini	7/–
☐ 552 07954 5	RUN FOR THE TREES	James Rand	7/–
☐ 552 08392 5	SOMETHING OF VALUE	Robert Ruark	8/–
☐ 552 08582 0	RAMAGE AND THE FREEBOOTERS	Dudley Pope	7/–
☐ 552 08584 7	THE BOUTIQUE OF THE SINGING CLOCKS	Lozania Prole	5/–
☐ 552 08372 0	LAST EXIT TO BROOKLYN	Hubert Selby Jr.	10/–
☐ 552 07807 7	VALLEY OF THE DOLLS	Jacqueline Susann	8/–
☐ 552 08523 5	THE LOVE MACHINE	Jacqueline Susann	8/–
☐ 552 08013 6	THE EXHIBITIONIST	Henry Sutton	7/6
☐ 552 08217 1	THE CARETAKERS	Dariel Telfer	7/–
☐ 552 08091 8	TOPAZ	Leon Uris	8/–
☐ 552 08383 4	EXODUS	Leon Uris	8/–
☐ 552 08563 4	THE KING'S MISTRESS	Julia Watson	4/–
☐ 552 08073 X	THE PRACTICE	Stanley Winchester	8/–
☐ 552 08391 7	MEN WITH KNIVES	Stanley Winchester	7/–
☐ 552 08581 2	DIONYSUS	Roderick Thorp	7/–

War

☐ 552 08565 0	BATTLE OF THE APRIL STORM	Larry Forrester	5/–
☐ 552 08551 0	ONE MAN'S WARS	Gilbert Hackforth-Jones	5/–
☐ 552 08552 9	CHINESE POISON	Gilbert Hackforth-Jones	5/–
☐ 552 08528 6	MARCH BATTALION	Sven Hassel	6/–
☐ 552 08587 1	SUBSMASH!	J. E. MacDonnell	5/–
☐ 552 08593 6	THE LONGEST DAY	Cornelius Ryan	6/–
☐ 552 98558 9	FOURTEEN EIGHTEEN (illustrated)	John Masters	21/–
☐ 552 08536 7	THE SCOURGE OF THE SWASTIKA (illus.)	Lord Russell	6/–
☐ 552 08537 5	THE KNIGHTS OF BUSHIDO (illustrated)	Lord Russell	6/–
☐ 552 08470 0	UNOFFICIAL HISTORY	Field-Marshal Sir William Slim	5/–
☐ 552 08527 8	THE LONG DROP	Alan White	5/–

Romance

☐ 552 08515 4	THE HEALING TIME	Lucilla Andrews	4/–
☐ 552 08569 3	ST. JULIAN'S DAY	Bess Norton	4/–
☐ 552 08477 8	A STRANGER IN TOWN	Alex Stuart	4/–

Science Fiction

☐ 552 08499 9	REACH FOR TOMORROW	Arthur C. Clarke	5/–
☐ 552 08516 2	NEW WRITINGS IN SF 17	John Carnell	5/–

All these books are available at your book shop or newsagent; or can be ordered direct from the publisher. Just tick the titles you want and fill in the form below.

CORGI BOOKS, Cash Sales Department, P.O. Box 11, Falmouth, Cornwall.

Please send cheque or postal order. No currency, and allow 9d. per book to cover the cost of postage and packing in U.K., 1/- per copy overseas.

NAME ....

ADDRESS ....

(DEC. 70) ....